Fabulous

"I think you've _____,"
she said.

"I'm really sorry you lost your wife, but *I'm not her.*"

Andrew made no move to follow her, but his voice rang clearly behind her. "Okay, you're not her. You just have her face, her eyes, her hair, her voice, and *her scar* on your chin."

She stopped. She did have a scar on her chin. She'd wondered a million times where it had come from.

"Laura, why did you leave?"

She couldn't answer him.

"Okay, forget me," Andrew said angrily. "Forget me altogether. How could you leave your child?"

Child!

Dear Reader,

This month, Silhouette Romance is celebrating the classic love story. That intensely romantic, emotional and compelling novel you just can't resist. And leading our month of classic love stories is *Wife without a Past* by Elizabeth Harbison, a deeply felt tale of an amnesiac wife who doesn't recognize the FABULOUS FATHER she'd married....

Pregnant with His Child... by bestselling author Carla Cassidy will warm your heart as a man is reunited with the child he never knew existed—and the woman he never stopped loving. Next, our MEN! promotion continues, as Silhouette Romance proves a good man isn't hard to find in *The Stranger's Surprise* by Laura Anthony. In Patricia Thayer's moving love story, *The Cowboy's Convenient Bride,* a woman turns up at a Texas ranch with a very poignant secret. And in *Plain Jane Gets Her Man* by Robin Wells, you'll be delighted by the modern-day Cinderella who wins the man of her dreams. Finally, Lisa Kaye Laurel's wonderful miniseries, ROYAL WEDDINGS, continues with *The Prince's Baby.*

As the Thanksgiving holiday approaches, I'd like to give a special thanks to all of you, the readers, for making Silhouette Romance such a popular and beloved series of books. Enjoy November's titles!

Regards,

Melissa Senate
Senior Editor
Silhouette Books

Please address questions and book requests to:
Silhouette Reader Service
U.S.: 3010 Walden Ave., P.O. Box 1325, Buffalo, NY 14269
Canadian: P.O. Box 609, Fort Erie, Ont. L2A 5X3

WIFE WITHOUT
A PAST

Elizabeth Harbison

Published by Silhouette Books

America's Publisher of Contemporary Romance

To the witches: Chris, Elaine, Mary,
Mary Kay, Nora and Pat.

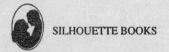 SILHOUETTE BOOKS

ISBN 0-373-19258-4

WIFE WITHOUT A PAST

Copyright © 1997 by Elizabeth Harbison

Printed in U.S.A.

Books by Elizabeth Harbison

Silhouette Romance

A Groom for Maggie #1239
Wife without a Past #1258

ELIZABETH HARBISON

has been writing fiction since elementary school, when she added sixty pages onto her copy of *Black Beauty*, bringing all the horses back to life. "Happily ever after" is a concept she takes seriously!

After publishing three cookbooks, Elizabeth decided to try her hand at writing romance. The rest, as they say... well, you know. Today, in addition to being a Silhouette author, she is an active member of the Washington chapter of the Romance Writers of America.

Elizabeth lives in Germantown, Maryland, with her husband, John, her daughter, Paige, and their dog, Bailey (who is named after George Bailey in *It's a Wonderful Life*).

Always one to appreciate comments and feedback on her work, Elizabeth loves to hear from readers. You can write to her c/o Silhouette Books, 300 E. 42nd Street, New York, NY 10017.

Dear Samantha,

Today is your mother's birthday. She's been gone for a little more than a year, but sometimes it seems like she just stepped out yesterday. And sometimes it feels like it's been forever.

I want to tell you about your mother, while it's still so fresh in my mind, but you're too young to understand it all right now. So I thought I'd write it down and give this to you when you're older.

Where do I start? Your mother was the most beautiful and intelligent woman I ever met. The day we got married, I truly felt like the luckiest man on earth. If she were here, she'd probably tell you that she chased me until I caught her—she used to say that all the time—but the truth is that the minute I laid eyes on her, I knew I wanted to spend the rest of my life with her.

You know, I'm finding that even as I write this, I feel strange talking about her in the past tense. In my mind I know she's gone, but, as crazy as it sounds, sometimes I could swear she's nearby. There are days when I even catch myself looking out the window at the front walk, as if it were just a matter of time before she came home....

Love,

Daddy

Chapter One

Laura!

Drew Bennett froze midstep on the sidewalk of Broad Street in Nantucket. His heart gave one mighty bang, like an ax cutting into solid oak, then fluttered, like leaves spiraling to the ground.

Impossible. Still, he didn't move. He couldn't move.

His eyes were fixed, practically burning, on a woman by the old bank building. It was her familiar stance that caught his eye first. In the midst of a crowd she looked untouchable. She was tall and slender—more slender than she'd been before—with a chin-length swish of glossy red hair. It used to be long, he thought vaguely. Past her shoulders. But that vibrant color was unmistakable.

Drew tried to see her face but it was difficult. The light breeze pushed tree shadows back and forth across her, alternately illuminating and hiding her face in darkness. He was too far away. But he was afraid to take a step toward her for fear that she would disappear, a spirit in the mist.

Again.

So he stayed at his vantage point, studying her. He didn't have a lot of experience with hallucinations, but it struck him as odd that he didn't recognize the clothes she wore. Faded jeans and a bright blue T-shirt that read *Ozone Or No Zone*. A threadbare green sweater was knotted around her waist.

The wind lifted again, and she raised her chin and flipped her hair back out of her eyes. His stomach lurched. It was a gesture he'd seen her do a thousand times before.

Laura. Drew swallowed hard and closed his eyes. It wasn't real. It couldn't be. It *felt* real, but his thundering heart, burning eyes and the chill grinding down his spine were *proof* of nothing. Surely it was all a figment of his weary imagination. But when he opened his eyes she was still there. Only ten yards away at the most. A memory, seeming to live and breathe like everyone around her. He could barely breathe.

She was looking at something in her hands. A street map? Of all people, she wouldn't need one. Drew squinted his eyes to see better. It *was* a street map. He frowned. Why would Laura—even his own hallucination of her—need a map of the town she'd lived in all her life?

His pounding heart gave no promise of calming, so he took a moment to gather some strength and moved toward her. One step. Still there. Two steps. She hadn't disappeared yet. She hadn't even moved. Three steps closer made him three times more positive that it was her.

No. It had to be a ghost.

Before he could take a fourth step, she turned away. Not vanished—turned away. He took a moment to catch his breath as she ambled up the street, pausing occasionally to look in a shop window. Drew followed, watching, slowly closing the gap between them. She stopped in front of Addy's Attic, a store featuring the paintings of local artists. Addy's had always been one of her favorite haunts. Now it appeared that was literally true. He watched for her usual enthusiasm to draw her in as it always did.

But as she stood there, her stature took on an odd stiffness. She pressed her lips together and leaned in, laying her hand to the window glass. Her stillness was unnerving. Then she gave a small shake of her head and walked away.

Moving with the slow hesitation of a dreamer, Drew continued following.

When she stopped at a bookshop a block up, there was no more than fifteen feet between the two of them, but he stopped, too. After what he'd been through since she'd…gone…he didn't want to take any chance of spooking her before getting some answers from her. *How can you be here? Can you speak? Can you hear?*

Can you stay?

A crowd of people milled around them. May was busy enough on Nantucket, but add lunch hour to the formula and you had a real mess. Drew had to step aside once or twice just to keep his eyes trained on her.

She must have felt his gaze because she turned suddenly and faced him.

Bam! It was a sucker punch to the gut. Even though

he knew the face well, the impact of seeing it, albeit from a slight distance, pulled his stomach straight into his empty lungs.

"It's you..." His voice trailed off and he reached an arm out toward her, even though she was too far away to reach, or to even hear him.

He realized quickly, though, that she wasn't looking at him but at something behind him. Her eyes seemed to search the crowd, as if she was looking for someone else, before she turned and walked away again.

Drew was dazed for a moment; then he moved to catch up with her. "Wait!" he called, but she only picked up her speed. "Laura!"

She didn't even turn around.

"Laura, answer me!" he yelled, heedless of the curious stares of passersby. "What's going on?"

A beefy hand grabbed his arm. "Looks like the lady wants to be left alone," a gruff voice cautioned.

Drew jerked his head toward the interloper. It was a construction worker. Part of the crew that was patching the sidewalk in an effort to keep the historic district in top form. His big face was seared a menacing red by the sun, and his forearm was the size of a small tree trunk.

Drew shrugged him off. "You saw her? A woman with red hair?"

The man's face went slack. "What are you, some sort of nut? Of course I saw her. I'm not blind."

Then she's real. She's not a figment of my imagination.

"Go home, buddy. Sleep it off." The worker walked off, shaking his head.

Drew barely heard him. The man's words had a

certain ring to them. *Was* she running away from him?

No, these thoughts were crazy. If she was a ghost, which she surely was, she would have better ways to get away than by running. And maybe she didn't realize he was calling to her. After all, the noise of the crowd created a dull roar.

Drew picked up his pace. She'd be glad to see him. Of course she would. He just had to catch up to her. He lost sight of her for a moment, then saw her again by the menu outside the Cobbler Restaurant.

"Laura! Here!" In three strides he was there, and turned her by the shoulders.

The woman who faced him was unfamiliar, and bore little likeness to Laura. For one thing, she couldn't have been older than twenty and she was shorter and a little on the plump side. The hair was similar to Laura's, the cut was the same, but nothing else was.

She smiled a big toothy grin at him and winked an amber eye. "My name's Gert," she said in a broad Australian accent. "Will I do?"

"I'm sorry," Drew said, trying to shake his mind clear. "I thought you were someone else." Was this the woman he'd been following for the past twenty minutes? Was he that far around the bend?

That was a more comfortable explanation than anything else he could come up with.

He flicked a glance across her. No, it wasn't the woman he'd seen. Gert wore a gauzy tie-dyed outfit one of the stores by the wharf was selling, not the jeans and T-shirt he'd seen Laura in. He gave a brief, distracted smile. "Sorry, my mistake."

"If you want to make another one, I'm staying at the Driftwood," the girl called after him.

He walked away, scanning the crowd for Laura. It wasn't long before he spotted her standing at the counter in the drugstore across the street, signing a check and tearing it out of the book.

Do ghosts write checks? The idea was so absurd that he immediately concluded that this was a person with an uncanny resemblance to Laura. Perhaps even a twin she'd never known about. Was that possible? No. A twin wouldn't have the same mannerisms unless they'd grown up together.

The corner traffic light turned green and a veritable stampede of cars roared out in front of him. Drew muttered an oath and searched for a gap in traffic to run through. It was bumper to bumper and moving fast. This time he shouted the oath. What was going on? Suddenly it was like rush hour in New York City.

Finally he got to the other side of the street, and he burst into the drugstore, the tiny bells on the door tingling a small, frantic announcement. He rushed to the crowded counter area.

She was gone.

He pressed through the customers in line and said to the bored-looking cashier, "There was a woman in here just now." He swallowed and tried to catch his breath. "A minute ago. Tall, red hair. Did you see which way she went?"

The cashier snorted. "Do I look like Sherlock Holmes?" A titter of laughter in the line brought a smug smile to her lips.

Drew tried to keep his voice sounding controlled. "This is important."

"I don't know where she went."

He braced his hands on the counter and raised his eyes skyward. Then it hit him. "She wrote a check."

The cashier nodded her gray head and settled back on her considerable haunches, a challenge clear in her eyes. "What about it?"

Drew tried to smile. "You won't believe this...." He reconsidered. Better not to sound like a lunatic. "I think that's someone I went to college with but I'm not sure it's her and I don't want to call all over town trying to find her if I've got the wrong woman."

She was not receptive. "Uh-huh."

"There's a line here, mister," a voice complained behind him.

"She just wrote a check," Drew persisted to the cashier. "Could you just take a look and see if it's the same woman?" Silence. "Her name is Amy," he tried to think of a last name and his eye fell on the cigarette display behind her, "Camela. Amy Camela." *You'll never be an actor, Bennett.*

"Amy Camela," the woman repeated dully.

By now his blood pressure had shot up to near-stroke level. "Please," he said through his teeth. He fumbled for his wallet and slipped a five-dollar bill out. He handed it to her, feeling like a bad actor in a bad movie. "Can you look at the check?"

Unbelievably, she relented and took the cash. For interminable moments she sifted through the cash drawer, then produced a plain beige check and read. "Nope. Says Mary Shepherd."

Well, what had he expected?

He'd expected Laura. He'd been so sure, so *completely* sure, that the cashier was going to say Laura Bennett that it took him a moment to comprehend what she *had* said. "Mary Shepherd?" he repeated, knowing as he spoke how insane his contention was. "You must have picked up the wrong check."

With that the cashier's patience reached its limit. "Look, fella, this is the only check I got today."

"Okay." He started to turn away, then turned back and asked, "Did you happen to notice if she was left-handed or right-handed?" Laura was left-handed. But what would finding out prove?

The cashier glared at him. "No." She looked behind him. "Next, please."

Drew stepped back. Mary Shepherd. This had to be a dream. A terribly realistic dream.

Or was he going insane?

Of course he was going insane. He'd just followed "Laura" across town. If that wasn't crazy, what was? Outside, he stopped by a strip of sidewalk shops and leaned against the warm stucco wall. He tilted his face toward the sun, then closed his eyes and heaved a sigh. Had it been some sort of mirage? Or had he invented the whole thing? That was seeming more and more possible.

Maybe he needed a vacation. He and Samantha could go someplace far away from Nantucket, far from the memories that haunted every street and alleyway. Samantha had been talking about going away anyhow. After seeing nothing but ocean all year round, she wanted to go to the mountains. Maybe that was just the break he needed.

He opened his eyes and glanced at his watch. One o'clock. One o'clock and no specters in sight. It was just an ordinary Wednesday afternoon. Might as well get back to work, he thought. *As if I can get anything done today.*

His gait back was slow and decidedly heavy. His

head ached, and his stomach was in knots. He was tired, he decided, not insane. Drew almost smiled to himself. Bennetts didn't go insane—his father never would have tolerated it.

By the time he got to the town house with the Biggins, Bennett and Holloway, Architects sign, he had just about convinced himself that he'd seen a woman that looked something like Laura and his imagination had conjured the rest. He was probably coming down with the flu and had experienced an elaborate hallucination.

Then he saw her again.

She was slipping some postcards into a mailbox not half a block away. This time there was no one else around her, and he got a good look. She was real, all right—and if nothing else, this Mary Shepherd had an extraordinary resemblance to Laura. He wondered again if she was a twin, but he couldn't believe Laura's overbearing mother could ever give up anything she considered hers. And she'd always considered Laura *hers.*

The woman held the last postcard back and took a pen out. She jotted something on it.

With her left hand.

"Hey!" Drew called to her in a voice that trembled. "Laura!"

She didn't even look at him. Instead, she raised her hand to stop a passing cab, and thrust the card at the mailbox, apparently without noticing it slip to the ground. She stepped into the street toward the car.

"Hey!" he called again.

She didn't pause, she didn't turn, she just opened the door and climbed in. As the car trundled toward him, he breathed her name one more time. She turned and looked straight at him. It was an arrow to the heart. Her face was as familiar to him as his own child's except for the utterly blank expression in her eyes.

It was more than blank, it was totally empty. No spark, no smile, no anger, nothing. No emotion at all. She was like a ghost—he went cold at the thought— or a shadow of a person from another time.

A chill—was it fear?—rattled through him.

"*Damn* it," he muttered as the car disappeared around a corner. Of all the things he would have imagined feeling at seeing Laura again, fear shouldn't have been on the list.

He went to the postcard on the ground and picked it up. His adrenal glands must have worn themselves out because, even as he studied the handwriting, certain it was Laura's, he was numb.

The card was addressed to a Nella Laraby in Litchfield, Connecticut.

Dear Nella,
Everyone was right, this island is heavenly. It's exactly the respite I needed. Thanks again for all your help. I can't wait to see you next week and tell you all about the trip.

Love to all,
Mary

Mary. Further proof that this was just a case of mistaken identity. Not a ghost, not a hallucination.

He looked back at the postcard, thinking maybe he should hold on to it as proof. But what did it prove? And who did he need to prove it to? It was handwriting, that was all, and signed by "Mary." No one would take it as proof that Laura was around. It even gave him doubts. Besides, he had no right to keep it. He opened the mailbox and dropped the card in.

Someone clapped a hand on his shoulder and Drew jumped.

"Whoa! Didn't mean to scare you, buddy," Drew's friend and co-worker Vince Reese said. "What's going on? What are you doing out here?"

Drew turned to face Vince, whose clownlike orange hair on his tall, lanky body was like a flame on a matchstick. "You wouldn't believe it if I told you. You'd think I was nuts. Hell, *I* think maybe I'm nuts."

"Try me."

Drew hesitated, then shrugged. "I just saw Laura."

There was a long silence.

"Laura?" Vince echoed at last.

Drew nodded and rubbed his eyes with his thumb and index finger.

"As in...*your* Laura?"

Drew tightened his lips and nodded. "Yup. Chased her all the way across town. Ready to commit me?"

Vince's screwed up his brow. "You just saw Laura. Uh-huh. What was she doing?"

"Window-shopping mostly." Drew thrust his hands into his pockets. "And then she went for a ride in a cab. So—" he puffed air into his cheeks, then blew it out "—ready to get back in to work?" He started to walk toward the office building.

Vince put a hand up to stop him. "You just saw Laura shopping and riding in a taxi and now you want to go back in to work?"

Drew raised his shoulders. "I considered chasing the cab but I'm not as fast as I used to be, you know.

I can hardly ever run fifty miles an hour anymore."
His flippant tone belied the trembling in his chest.

Vince shook his head and fell in step beside Drew.
"I don't get this. Is it April Fool's Day?" He looked
at his watch. "No, it's May. What's going on, man?
Do you need a visit with the old head shrinker, or are
you pulling a joke on me?"

"Neither." Drew clapped Vince on the shoulder.
"I saw a woman who looked just exactly like Laura.
Exactly. But she slipped away before I got a chance
to see her up close." *Or I let her slip away,* he
thought. *I let her slip away all afternoon because I
was afraid to know for sure one way or the other.*

"But you do know it couldn't have been Laura. I
mean, it's been more than a year since—"

"A year and three months." Drew nodded. "I
know. I haven't totally lost my mind. It was obviously
a case of mistaken identity."

"That's it." Vince's voice was just a little bit too
patronizing.

Drew ignored it. "I probably just need a good long
rest. I thought maybe Samantha and I would go up to
Vermont for a while."

"That's not such a bad idea," Vince said. "You've
always been a major workaholic, but over the past
year you've been killing yourself working here *and*
at home. Tell you what, I'll go with you guys. How
about Disney World?"

Drew stopped. "I appreciate the offer, but I was
thinking of the mountains. Samantha's been making
noise about seeing them." He sighed, thinking about
her, then shook his head. "I owe her something special. She's the most precious thing in my life. If it

weren't for her, I don't know what I would have done this past year.''

Vince gave him a dismissive slap on the back. ''Well, you got through it, man.'' Obviously he was eager to brush Drew's momentary lapse in sanity under the carpet.

Did I? ''I guess I did.''

''And today you just saw someone who looked a lot like Laura. Not actually Laura herself.'' Vince tried to give a little laugh, but it sounded to Drew more like a dismissive cough. ''Because, you know...''

''I know.'' Their eyes met. Yes, Drew knew. He knew all too well. He'd had more than a year to get used to the idea, to accept it and go on with his life.

Laura Bennett, his beautiful young wife and the mother of little Samantha, had been dead and buried for more than a year.

Chapter Two

The rest of the day passed slowly for Drew. He got nothing done in the way of work. Instead, he spent most of his time looking out the window at the breezy May afternoon. The brilliant sun shining through the old mottled window threw prisms of color across the floor.

He could picture the exact color of Laura's hair in sun like this—it was the color of a copper penny, gleaming as if newly minted. And her eyes, almond shaped, were the palest of blue. Not the emerald green of Irish stereotype, but blue like the sky on a clear summer morning.

It wasn't her, he told himself. *It couldn't have been. That's impossible.* But the truth was he found it harder to believe it *wasn't* her. He'd never been one to experience hallucinations or to imagine things. And his eyesight was perfect, though he was hardly likely to assume someone was Laura, no matter how great the similarity, without some good solid detail.

He closed his stinging eyes tightly, then opened them and looked out the window again. He couldn't stop picturing Laura in the sunny spring day. It had taken more than a year to stop thinking of her every hour of every day. Now there was a look-alike out there somewhere. It made him want to barricade himself in his house and never go out again, never take a chance on seeing that woman—whoever she was— again. He wasn't sure he could survive another delve into that sort of grief.

He wasn't the only one who couldn't go through it again. His eyes fell on a picture on his desk. It was a little girl with auburn hair and blue eyes, smiling into the camera and right into his heart. Samantha, his daughter. Sam, Laura had called her. Like in *Green Eggs and Ham*, the Dr. Seuss book. "I do not like green eggs and ham, I do not like them, Sam I am."

He could still hear Laura's musical voice, like a ghost in the hall, reciting the words.

He remembered every word of the book even though he hadn't picked it up since the day of the accident. She'd left it on the kitchen table after reading it to Sam at breakfast. When he'd come home that afternoon, after a tinny voice on the telephone had informed him that she'd been killed in a crash on I-95 just over the Connecticut state line, the book had still been sitting open on the kitchen table.

For some reason, that had struck him as proof that she was coming back. It was all a bad dream, of course. Laura was coming back; she hadn't finished reading *Green Eggs and Ham* to Sam. It was impossible to imagine that she wouldn't come back and pick it up right where she'd left off. And something in his mind told him that if he just left the book there, didn't touch it, she would come back to it.

That had only lasted a few hours, though. When he came back from the coroner's office in Connecticut late that night, his secretary, Mindy, had already tidied up and put the book back on the bookshelf with hundreds of others. That small fact alone had clinched it for him. The spell of shock and disbelief that had suspended his grief was broken.

Laura was dead. She'd walked out on him without warning or explanation early one February morning. That alone was baffling enough, but she hadn't just left Drew, she'd also left their three-year-old daughter behind. She'd read the book to her, taken her to preschool and then kept on driving. It was so unlike Laura that to this day he couldn't figure it in to his acceptance of her death.

But during those last few months, she'd done a lot of things he would have thought were unlike her. And there were insecurities, accusations, suspicions. He'd realized she was upset, but he'd had no idea she was upset enough to leave her family.

But she had. And only hours later she was pronounced dead in a hospital two hundred miles away. There was never an opportunity for explanations or restitution.

The long months had plodded by to the present. Drew's eyes focused on the picture of Sam again. He often wondered just how much she remembered about her mother. She'd been so young when it had happened—barely three. At first she'd felt the loss constantly. It had been hell having to explain to her over and over again that, no, Mommy wasn't coming back. Sam seemed to think that was a concept that had flexibility. Mommy wasn't home one day but maybe the next—when she really wanted to show her a new drawing—she would be back.

Drew picked up a pen and started sketching absently on the ink blotter in front of him.

Gradually Sam's memories seemed to have faded. Now she merely asked questions about Laura. What was she like? Was she nice? Was she pretty? Drew never knew if she'd truly bounced back and lost those young memories, or if she didn't remember because she didn't want to remember.

Just like Drew didn't want to. Because remembering was too painful.

He added a couple of lines to his sketch. A cloud. He couldn't blame Laura for leaving, though. Not entirely. He'd had a lot of time to think about it, and had realized many regrets of his own. There were too many things he should have said but didn't. Perhaps worse, there were too many things he shouldn't have said but did. Sometimes he felt he was as responsible for her death as the car accident had been.

If he had it to do over again, he would have done things so differently.

But he didn't have things to do over again. That had been the hardest lesson to learn over the past year; he had to accept that she wasn't coming back and that his regrets were useless.

Drew looked back down at what he'd been doodling. It was a very rough sketch of the children's beach, near the Port Authority. He added a few lines to the water. Laura had always liked to go there and watch the boats come and go. He hadn't been there in months, hadn't even thought about it until now. Of course, he hadn't drawn anything other than lines and angles in as long, either. He started to sketch her into the picture, then slapped the pen down on the desk.

Laura was dead, and like the rest of the dead population, she was going to stay that way. He had to accept it.

Mary Shepherd fingered the ring on the street vendor's cart. It was an Irish Claddagh ring. She knew because one of the women at the shelter had worn one when she'd arrived. She'd come in with it symbolizing attachment to a man who abused her. By the time she'd left, healed and renewed, she'd turned it to symbolize a woman alone. The ring and its meanings had always appealed to Mary in some strange way that she couldn't quite name.

Of course, there were a lot of things Mary couldn't quite name. Herself, not the least of them.

For a year now she'd been Mary Shepherd because she'd woken up in St. Joseph's Memorial Hospital in Connecticut with a horrendous head wound, rope burns on her wrists and ankles and no memory of how any of it had happened. No memory of her life before. She wore no wedding ring, but her left ring finger was creased as though she'd worn a ring there for a long time and only taken it off recently. But she didn't even know her name, much less what sort of ring she might have worn.

"Psychogenic amnesia," the doctors had called it. Her reaction to a trauma so great she couldn't bear to remember it. Could last a month, could last forever. There was no way to tell.

Mary's money was on forever. Because in fifteen months she'd had no memory—good or bad, recent or distant—beyond small instinctive pulls. Like the one that had brought her to Nantucket. She had such an affinity for water that the women at the shelter where she lived and worked had teased that she was probably a navy captain in charge of hundreds of men at sea, and who wouldn't want to forget that? But when she'd seen the pictures of Nantucket in the travel agent's window, she'd known that she *had* to see it in person. It had to be Nantucket, not Cape Cod, not Bayville, but Nantucket.

So her co-workers had pooled their money and sent her north on a bus. A well-deserved rest, they called it, for the hardest worker at Sisters Anonymous.

She looked back at the ring. Turn it one way, you're one thing. Slip it off and turn it around and you're something else altogether. Maybe that was why it had always appealed to her. The idea that she could just turn a magic ring around and be the person she was before the accident would have been so wonderful.

Sam I am. The odd little phrase came to her, as it sometimes did, without warning or explanation. *Sam I am.* She'd twisted it around and analyzed it every way possible. Was her name Sam? Was there a man in her life named Sam? Did the letters stand for something else? It had even occurred to her that she might have been in the armed services, thinking of "Uncle Sam," but none of that seemed right.

The sun glinted in her eyes from the silver in her finger. Yes, magic would be wonderful whether it was in the ring or in the air. Too bad it didn't exist. She set the ring back in its place on the cart, looked at it for a moment and asked the vendor, "How much?"

The wizened old proprietor scratched his chin. "For you, ten dollars."

She smiled. Most of the pieces there were marked ten dollars. "Will you take five?" He hesitated and she added, "It's all I have and...I really want the ring." She didn't have a lot of money and virtually no budget for extras like this, but the magic she'd attributed to the ring didn't seem as absurd as it should have. When she'd slipped it on her finger, she'd had the feeling that something exciting was about to happen.

"I could never resist a pretty face," the man said, accepting her money.

She slipped the ring on and marveled at the comfortable way it settled at the base of her finger. In some small way it made her feel a little more whole. It was like another piece in the puzzle this week on Nantucket had become.

As she walked down Federal Street, she listened intently to her inner voice, trying to hear some tiny murmur of recognition, some small explanation of why it had brought her to Nantucket. But there was nothing beyond a strange feeling of comfort and safety in the quaint, winding streets and tall, narrow houses.

She stopped in front of a linen shop and looked at a children's bunk bed in the window. Something stirred inside of her. Her eyes scanned the other objects for something else that might make her stomach do that small flip. Then she realized the feeling had come not from what she was looking at but from the fact that someone was looking at her. Someone at her side.

She turned her head sharply and caught the eye of a tall, thin man with vivid red hair sticking straight up and out. His wide pale eyes stared at her as if she were a ghost. His mouth was agape.

For a moment, her heart pounded with terror, then she glanced at the throngs of people milling around them, and relaxed. *Safety in numbers.* When she looked back at him, his face was unchanged. Clearly he was just an unbalanced person, she decided.

She gave him a polite half smile, then cast her eyes down and walked farther down the sidewalk. The feeling that he was following her clung to her back like a cold, wet towel. Every once in a while she was tempted to stop at a shop window, but she kept catching glimpses of the man in the corner of her eye, following her with that comical expression of some sort of shock on his face.

A thought came to her, so absurd that she tried to dismiss it. But she couldn't. Was it possible that he recognized her? She met his eyes but his expression didn't change. He didn't move to speak to her, which he surely would have if he knew her. Instead, he just stared with that weird expression.

Good Lord, did he recognize her for some dark reason? Was she on a *wanted* poster in the Nantucket post offices? Had she done something terrible, then returned to the scene? Was she, even now, frightening the citizens as she passed?

No! The word echoed within her like the voice of a guardian angel. She hadn't done anything criminal, she knew it. Of course, she had no facts to back her up, no alibi for anything before awakening in the hospital, but she just knew she wasn't wanted for any crime. The very idea was laughable.

This guy following her was just some nutcase. As soon as he looked away, Mary slipped into one door of a corner kite store, and out the other. Best to stay away from nutcases. Just before she ran down the alley to lose him, she saw him enter the store. She hesitated only for a moment to see the top of that fuzzy orange head as he milled slowly down the aisle behind a tall display shelf.

Then she ran.

The doorbell rang, startling Drew out of the work he was trying so hard to submerge himself in. Somehow he thought it would be easier to work at his home office after the shake-up of "seeing" Laura, but the truth was the only thing he could submerge himself in was thoughts of her. The doorbell rang again.

He looked up, trying for one irrational moment to place the sound, then got up from his desk and walked to the front door, stopping along the way to pick up a stuffed frog that was in his path. Sam was going to a friend's house after preschool. The baby-sitter wasn't planning to bring her home until after dinner.

When he opened the door, he was surprised to see Vince standing there. His flaming orange hair was in its usual state of disarray, but his skin was ghostly white, with every freckle standing out on his skin like a fleck of dark paint. Alarm zinged in his eyes.

Drew's adrenaline surged. "What's wrong?" The stuffed frog flattened in his grip.

"Nothing." Vince glanced behind Drew and gestured. "Can I come in? We've got to talk."

Drew's heart accelerated. "Sure, come in." He stepped back and led the way through to the kitchen, tossing the frog onto the sofa as they passed.

"Coffee?" Drew offered.

Vince gave a shake of his head. "How are you feeling, man? All right?"

"Fine, Vince." A clammy feeling of trepidation crawled up Drew's spine. "Just fine." He knew, even though his soul rattled with incredulity, what Vince was going to tell him. After long seconds, he found his voice. "What's up?"

Vince scraped a chair back from the table and sat heavily. "Why don't you sit down?"

"I don't need to sit down." Drew leaned against the countertop and folded his arms across his throbbing chest. He studied his friend for a few moments before saying, "You saw her today, didn't you?"

There was no need to ask who they were talking about. Vince nodded.

Drew let out a tight breath. "Tell me."

"I'm sorry, man. When we talked before I really thought you were going nuts. I mean—" he twirled his finger outside of his temple "—Cloud Cuckoo Land, but now—"

"Where was she?"

"Federal Street. Thereabouts."

"Did you get a good look at her?" Drew asked. "I mean a *really* good look?"

"Well, you know, I felt I should be subtle. I just sort of blended into the crowd and followed her. That's how the pros do it. I saw her from three feet away. It was definitely her."

"Did she see you?"

There was a pause. "She saw me once. But she didn't talk to me. Didn't even act like she knew who I was. Just gave me a polite smile then walked past and sort of hurried down the street." Vince frowned and shook his head.

Drew's chest felt as though it was being crushed in a vise. How long could he have this feeling before it developed into a real honest-to-God heart attack? "Where did she go?"

"That's the other odd thing. She went into a kite store then just vanished. I followed her in, but she was gone. Like a gho..." He stopped and bit down on his lower lip.

"What time was this?" Even to his own ears, Drew sounded like Jack Webb from the TV show "Dragnet," but he couldn't manage more than a few direct questions.

Vince shrugged. "Just half an hour ago at the most."

Drew raked a trembling hand through his hair and stood up. "I've got to go." It was her. Logic be damned, he *knew* it was her.

"Whoa, buddy, better let me drive." Vince stood, as well. "You're in no state to get behind the wheel."

Drew met Vince's eyes with more impatience than he intended. "No." He tried to soften his voice but there didn't seem to be time. If Laura was alive and on Nantucket—hell, even if she was a ghost—he knew where she'd go eventually. "I've got to do this alone." Without giving Vince a moment to respond, he turned, snatched his car keys from the table by the door and left the house.

Mary looked around at the practically empty street she'd turned onto. Even though she'd felt as if she'd been walking in circles on the tiny Nantucket streets, she knew she hadn't been to this one before. Yet it seemed vaguely familiar, like something from a distant dream. To the right were quaint storefronts, to the left a long border of water, with boats gliding across the glassy surface. The sun was shining, a warm breeze carried the faint scent of saltwater, and in the distance the long expanse of water sparkled like jewels on blue velvet. She hadn't felt this alive, this *comfortable,* in fifteen months.

Her whole life.

She knotted her sweater around her shoulders, slipped her espadrilles off and ambled down the street swinging them in her hands. The pavement was warm beneath her feet. The atmosphere was delicious. She didn't think about where she was going, so she was surprised when she found herself on a lovely little square beach that looked out onto the ferry boats. Children ran all around her, squealing and laughing in the warm golden sand. In the summer, the beach was probably crowded with brightly colored towels and rubber floats.

She wanted to be here in the summer. She wanted to see that.

An empty wooden park bench sat in front of a colorful jungle gym and Mary sat down and closed her eyes, tilting her face toward the sun. Kaleidoscope patterns played behind her closed eyelids, forming and unforming, never quite becoming memory.

She didn't know how long she sat like that, but when she opened her eyes again, the sun had shifted its position and shadows had lengthened across the sand. There were fewer children out playing, but the light still danced warmly on her skin. She thought about getting up, but there was something so peaceful about this place that she had to breathe it in, just a little bit longer.

Then he came into view.

A man, perhaps six feet tall, with glossy chestnut hair and piercing eyes of a color she couldn't see, was walking slowly toward her. For a crazy second, she had an impulse to call out to him. It was an irrational impulse, she mused. Like one you'd follow in a dream.

Something shivered up her spine. *This isn't a dream. He's not going to turn into a crow and fly away. He's coming toward me. No, he's not,* she told herself. *Why would he be coming to me?*

He continued his even stride toward her. As he got closer, she noticed that his deep brown eyes changed from piercing to something else. A combination of emotions mingled in his expression, each with its own unmistakable distinction. She wasn't sure why she felt she could read them, but she was sure she could.

He stopped directly before her and stared down into her eyes for a long moment.

She pulled her sweater tighter across her shoulders and stood up, looking back at him. She thought she should say something, but she couldn't think of one word that would have made sense. Her eyes darted to the right, where a woman lay on a blanket on the sand with two small children at her heels. A few yards away from that, a teenage boy and girl were having what looked like a young lovers' spat.

She turned back to the stranger before her. Something about his expression was compelling, but she figured that under the circumstances she would be safer just getting away from him. She gave a polite smile and said, "Excuse me."

She started to brush past, when he grasped her upper arm and spun her around to face him.

They were inches apart. His eyes were lined faintly

with red, making him look more tragic than threatening. Mary's breath caught in her throat, but for some reason the terror she expected didn't reach her.

A small muscle twitched on the side of his clenched jaw, as if he were keeping some emotion in close check.

She stood frozen, mesmerized by his eyes, as he lifted his other hand to her shoulder and slowly pulled her toward him. Why wasn't she afraid? Any reasonable person would be hightailing it out of there, but she didn't move. The pounding of her heart felt more like excitement than fear.

His hand slipped around to her shoulder blade. The movement was hypnotic, almost as if it were familiar to her. She knew exactly what was next. She saw it coming like a locomotive but was powerless to stop it.

She didn't want to stop it.

He pulled her to him and his mouth descended onto hers. The touch of his lips was a spark. When he deepened his kiss and she felt his tongue probe her mouth, the spark became a raging flame. With an instinct wholly unfamiliar to her, she closed her eyes and raised her hands to the back of his head, tangling her fingers in his thick, dark hair.

This was a dance her body knew, even if her mind didn't.

She felt his shuddering breath on her skin, and her body echoed it. He ran his hands down her sides, slipped them around to her lower back and crushed her to him. Their bodies pressed together like palms in a handshake. Mary drew in a breath and released it in a sigh. His powerful embrace made her feel as if she was finally in exactly the right place.

Which was crazy, she knew, but it was also too comfortable to fight.

His mouth moved over hers, reacting to her movements in a practiced way. Everything felt *right*. Like the last piece clicking easily, triumphantly, into a puzzle.

Except that it wasn't right, it was wrong. This was a stranger! She had to stop.

"Stop!" Mary pulled back with some effort. "What do you think you're doing?" Her voice was too breathy to be commanding. "That's assault!" *Maybe, but on whose part? Why did I do that?*

"I thought I'd lost it when I saw you yesterday," the man said in a husky voice that made her insides quiver. "I thought I was nuts, but it *was* you."

Yesterday. What was yesterday? Had they met before? Was that why he seemed familiar? Mary concentrated and remembered. This was the man who watched her drive past in the cab. The only reason she remembered was because the way he'd looked at her had made her feel so peculiar. She'd had a crazy impulse to tell the driver to take her back so she could talk to the man. But she had nothing to say to him. Then or now.

Her eyes returned to the man before her and she found her voice. "I think you must have me confused with someone else." There. That was a nice comfortable explanation. He wasn't a maniac—maniacs didn't kiss like that.

Of course that didn't explain why *she'd* indulged so thoroughly in the kiss.

All the emotions fell from his face except one— sadness. Anyone could have identified it. His eyelids dipped and he shook his head and uttered a single low word. A name. "Laura."

The tiny hairs on the back of her neck prickled. Why?

"I—I'm sorry—"

"Are you real?"

"Am I *real?*" Where was the fear she should have felt at this strange and intense exchange? Why wasn't she running by now? "I'm as real as you are." She considered. "Maybe more."

"But—the body. I saw the body."

This was getting creepy. "I don't know what you're talking about. Now if you'll excuse me, I see my friend waiting for me over there." She gestured vaguely toward a group of people. Her voice, which was supposed to be confident, was as weak as a child's. She looked into his eyes to see if he'd noticed her lack of conviction.

"Laura... How can this be happening?" He looked lost, she thought. Lost. Utterly defenseless. She knew how that felt.

"My name is Mary Shepherd," she said, like that would clear up all the confusion. "I'm visiting from Connecticut."

"Mary Shepherd?" He repeated the name as if repeating a foreign language on an audiotape. He gave a humorless spike of laughter. "No, you're not. You're home."

The simplicity with which he stated it almost made her laugh. Almost. Instead, she felt her breath catch in her throat. *Home,* he'd said. *You're home.* A slow tingle moved down the back of her neck.

"I'm...not Mary Shepherd?" She tried to smile but it was tremulous at best. "And who do you think I am, then?'' It was meant to sound light, as though *of course* she knew who she was and this man was a fool if he thought she was someone else. But the possibility that he knew more than she did was just too real. A thin vibration ran through her chest, like a single violin note strung out to a trembling finish.

Maybe he *knew* who she was.

''Is this a joke?'' he asked, his tone rising.

Ridiculous, she thought. *He doesn't know who I am. He's just a madman. Evidently Nantucket is full of them.*

''Are you kidding?'' he prodded. His brown eyes searched hers desperately.

It was the desperation that spooked her the most. She had to get away. ''Am I laughing?'' She took a step back.

He laid a hand on her shoulder and she could feel it shaking. It was like fifty thousand volts running through him to her. ''Laura! What the hell is going on?''

She looked around for help—a policeman, anything. A psychiatrist.

''Laura!''

His pleading exclamation turned her attention back to him. She straightened her back. ''I told you, I'm not—''

''Good Lord, do you think I don't know my own wife when I see her?''

A blow to the gut couldn't have impacted her more.

He continued in a softer voice. ''My God, Laura, it really *is* you.''

She stood frozen, looking at him. ''You're mistaken.''

''Do you think I could possibly forget? Your hair.''

His fingers tickled through the shoulder-length ends of her hair. "It's shorter but the same color."

A tickle skirted her neck and, for reasons she couldn't begin to understand, she imagined him kissing her there.

"And your face." His thumb traced a burning line across her cheekbone. "My God, do you think I could forget that face? It's been over a year, but there wasn't a day I didn't think about it—"

Over a year. Her eyes closed and she fought the urge to lean into his touch.

"Your mouth." He traced the line of her lips with his finger.

Without thinking, she parted her lips and his finger nearly touched the tip of her tongue. A lightning bolt shot straight into the pit of her stomach. He caught her eye and cocked his head slightly. The movement was small, but meaningful. Familiar? No. But electrifying.

He put his finger to his own lips, then dropped his hand as if he'd touched something white-hot. "I thought I would die without you."

She swallowed but a hard lump remained in her throat. When her voice came out it was barely more than a whisper. "What—what happened to your wife?"

He lowered his brow and a hardness returned to his eyes. "*Great* question. Why the hell did you let me believe—let all of us believe—that you were dead?"

Suddenly she remembered coming to at St. Joseph's. The thundering head injury. The doctors had said that someone had hit her. It had taken a full year to grow the hair back to a decent length after the surgery. And the rope burns on her wrists and ankles, burns that had burrowed right through her flesh and left scars she could see to this day. She couldn't ignore the obvious question.

Had Laura wanted this man to find her? Or had she fled him to save herself—only to end up losing herself completely?

The thought was terrifying in its blindness. She pressed past the man whom, only a moment ago, she'd felt desire for. "I think you've got the wrong person," she said. She had to find a place to be alone and think. "I'm really sorry you lost your wife, but I'm not her."

He made no move to follow her, as far as she could tell, but his voice rang clearly behind her. "Okay, you're not her. You just have her face, her eyes, her hair, her voice, and her *scar* on your chin."

She stopped, but didn't turn back. Her heart was banging so ferociously, she was sure he could hear it eight feet away. She *did* have a scar on her chin; it had always been there. She'd wondered a million times where it came from. Without really thinking, she raised her fingers to the small bumpy spot.

He spoke again, but he hadn't made a move toward her. "Laura, why did you come back if you were going to hide from me?" He let out an exasperated sigh. "Never mind that, why did you leave?"

She didn't answer. She couldn't.

"Okay, forget me." She heard him take two or three steps toward her on the pavement. "Forget me altogether. How could you leave your child?"

Child!

Her knees went weak. It had never occurred to her that she might have children. That seemed like something a mother couldn't forget no matter what happened to her. Her heart twisted inside out and she thought for a moment she might get sick. Then she turned, very slowly, to face him.

"Child?" she repeated faintly.

He gave a curt nod, his eyes mere slits. "Or had you forgotten—"

"As a matter of fact I had."

"That, along with the rest of your family?" He stopped and frowned. "What did you say?"

"I said..." She swallowed. She didn't know who she *was* but she believed she never would have left a child behind with a physically abusive man. "Well, anyway, I *meant* that if I am this Laura you're talking about, then I *have* forgotten. I've forgotten everything. There was...an accident." She smiled but it felt like baring her teeth.

His featured hardened. "And you've forgotten Sam as well as me?"

Sam! The word hit her like a slap across the face. Could this be the Sam she'd been trying to recall? It had to be. Her heart raced. "Sam? Do I—do you— have a little boy?"

"What are you talking about? Sam? Samantha is your *daughter*."

Her breath caught in her throat. Daughter. Sam was her daughter.

"Laura? What's going on here?"

She returned her gaze to him, still barely able to breathe. "That name...I've..." She stopped, realizing how difficult it would be to explain when she herself understood so little. "I'm afraid I don't remember you, either."

He lowered his chin, considering, then seemed to dismiss the thought. "What are you talking about?

Amnesia?" he scoffed. Then he muttered, "That's a hell of an excuse."

"It's not an excuse," she said. Why would she need an excuse to not find her identity? Her eyes began to burn. Sam. Finally one fact in the months of confusion was starting to make sense. She wanted to spill her whole story and have him fill in all the missing pieces. She wanted to *remember.* But she didn't know this man from...from any other and, without really knowing anything about him, she would have to be an idiot to tell him she was a woman, alone, with no real identity.

"Maybe you can tell me why you're so convinced I'm Laura," she said. It was a pathetic attempt at detached curiosity.

"Tell you? How about I show you?" He whipped his wallet out of the back pocket of his jeans and fumbled through it until he produced a small stack of photos and handed them to her.

Some of them were wallet-size portraits, some snapshots, but all of them had one thing in common. They were unmistakably her. Her with him; her in a graduation cap and gown; her with a blond woman on the beach, in a pink swimsuit; her smiling and resting her hand on her own pregnant belly; and one of her holding hands with a small girl....

"Oh my God," she whispered. She ran her finger across the little girl in the picture. She had light auburn hair that gleamed in the light of the flash. Her eyes were wide and clear blue, and her uninhibited smile was pure happiness. She was a beautiful child.

Oh, how she would have missed her if she were her child, Mary thought. "How old is she?"

He hesitated. "Sam is four."

So young. She needed her mother still, but was that Mary? It was difficult to fathom. "She's lovely."

"I agree."

She met his eyes. "I'll bet she's sweet."

"She's the greatest kid ever." He laughed harshly. "Come on, Laura, you *know* that."

"I know that," she echoed without recollection. After another moment, she slipped the photo to the back of the pile and removed the graduation picture of Laura. She examined it closely. The scar on her chin was clearly visible, even a little bigger than it was now. She raised her hand to her chin again, then turned to him.

"How did I get it? The scar, I mean."

"You fell off a horse," he answered slowly, studying her with a different look now.

"I ride?"

"No." He was looking so deeply into her eyes that she felt naked. A tiny smile played at the corner of his mouth. "Not very well." The smile disappeared. "You know that."

"No, I don't."

He cocked his head to one side. "Come on."

"That's fairly cynical."

"I'm not a fool."

She smiled wanly. "Then do I bring out this cynicism in you?"

"I'm not cynical," he protested. "I'm wary. You always did have a way of blowing things way out of proportion. Are you trying to tell me you don't remember *anything?* Nothing at all? Not your name? Your first dog's name? Zero?"

"I remember what I had for breakfast this morning,

and where I bought my shoes, but I can't remember anything beyond the last year or so.''

He opened his mouth, then closed it and shifted his weight. When he spoke again, his voice registered absolute bemusement. ''This isn't a put-on? You honestly have some sort of amnesia or something? Does that really happen?''

She paused and studied him with the impartial eye she'd developed at Sisters Anonymous. ''You've got a lot of questions, but let me ask you one.'' *One that might answer a lot of questions about what happened to me and why, if I'm your wife, I've spent the last year with no identity, hundreds of miles away.* She kept her gaze steady. ''Is your wife the kind of person who would lie to you?''

Chapter Three

He eyed her steadily without speaking at first. "My wife," he said slowly, "is the kind of person who was so scared to trust the people who loved her that she turned away from them."

"From them? Or from you?"

"From all of us. Especially from me." He swallowed. "She was so sure that I didn't love her that she distanced herself from me. To protect herself from the pain of...I guess of losing me." He looked hard into her eyes. "Isn't that crazy?"

He was obviously expecting her to take umbrage. "Maybe so, but that sort of thing doesn't usually happen without a good reason."

"A good reason," he scoffed. "You mean like having parents who didn't love each other and who didn't *trust* each other? I'm sorry I don't think that's a good reason to re-create that atmosphere for your own daughter. I don't think that's a good reason to treat your husband like a criminal because he doesn't..." He shook his head. "I don't think that's a good reason to retreat from your life so much that you eventually have to fake your own death in order to be alone."

"Hey, maybe your wife had reasons to try and get away from you and maybe she didn't, but *I* don't know anything about that."

"Laura, this is insane!"

"If this is truly me we're talking about," she began in a cold tone, noting how absurd her words were, "then I'm telling you for the last time, *I don't remember*. All I know is that I woke up in a hospital a year ago with no idea who or where I was, and I've had to struggle through worse hell than you've probably ever known to try and make sense of it."

They stood face-to-face like boxers. Then she added, "And if you cared so stinking much about me, how is it that you never came to find me?"

"Because you were dead!"

She splayed her arms and looked down at herself. "Apparently not."

"I *thought* you were."

"Oh, I see. You *thought* I was. Well, that's good enough. That makes up for it." She shook her head. "If that's the sort of dumb faith you expected of your wife, then no wonder you thought she didn't trust enough. Who could?"

"It wasn't dumb faith. Your car was wrecked, there was a body wearing your jewelry, your *wedding* ring." His voice weakened over those words. "All your identification was there."

"Did you identify the body?"

"Yes—no. I mean, it was burnt beyond recognition."

"Did you check the dental records?" She noticed how defensive she sounded, but she couldn't help it. She felt a little sorry for him, but she felt even sorrier, not for herself, but for the woman she had apparently been.

The woman who had been allowed to disappear as "dead" when she was alive and struggling to go from day to day.

"No," he answered. "It didn't seem necessary to check the dental records."

She raised an eyebrow. "Did you check the hospitals and police stations for Jane Does in the area?"

"Of course not. We thought we had you!" He was clearly losing patience.

So was she. "Then that's dumb faith."

He thumped his head with his palm. "God, if that isn't just like you. You know there are *two* sides to this, not just yours. Don't you think if there had been an *ounce* of doubt, I would have investigated? No, of course you don't. You never did think I loved you."

"*Obviously* there was reason enough to investigate further." She shrugged, but his words had thrown her. *You never did think I loved you.* "If I'm Laura, I mean."

"I give." He shook his head, and let out a long breath. "I can't argue with that. But who would believe this?"

"I have no choice but to believe it," she said simply.

He was obviously still wrestling with believing her. "It's just so farfetched. Amnesia?"

She folded her arms in front of her. It was a classic self-defense mechanism and she knew it. "You want my medical history?"

"Yes."

She considered this for a moment. "Me, too."

He almost laughed, but sobered quickly. "What am I supposed to say, Laura? What do we do?"

She straightened. "I don't have a lot of experience with this, either."

When neither of them spoke, she said, "Let's try this again. I guess we should get acquainted. I don't even know your name." She shook her head. "I'm sorry, but…"

"Drew," he said. "Bennett. Drew Bennett. You're—you're Laura Bennett." He looked around. "This is unbelievable," he muttered under his breath.

"If you want unbelievable, try stepping into my shoes."

"I can't. We gave them all away after you died."

She smiled and felt some of the tension slip away.

He reached a hand out to her. "Oh, Laura, I can't believe this. I just can't believe it. Tell me you're not a ghost."

She handed his pictures back to him. "That much I know. I'm not a ghost."

"Or a dream?"

"Or a dream."

He looked skyward. "Thank you. Thank you so much." He returned his gaze to her.

A tingle shot up her spine and she realized, with some impatience, that she hoped he'd take her into his arms again. She wanted one more of those delicious kisses, like one more helping of dessert. But whether she once did or not, she didn't know this man anymore.

He drew a breath in through his teeth. "Let's— uh—can we—go someplace? Try to figure this out?"

He put the pictures back into his wallet. "How about Arno's?"

Arno's. Why did she know that name? Then she remembered; she'd passed it earlier. The menu was tempting but expensive and she was on a limited budget. She looked down at her purse, then back at him. "Maybe someplace simpler."

He followed her gaze to her purse, then looked her in the eye. "You can't be worried about money."

"Why not?"

He gave a brief, exasperated laugh. "Because—" He tapped his wallet and smiled before putting it back in his pocket. "Family bank account."

"I can't accept that."

His jaw dropped. "How much more proof do you need? What's it going to take for you to accept your own identity?"

"I meant I can't accept your money," she said quietly.

"Ah." His face colored faintly. "It's your money, too."

"Okay. Then I don't want to spend it on me."

"Would you, for just once in your life, please accept something from someone else without turning it into some huge emotional mortgage?"

Laura paused, remembering the words of a coworker just a few days before. *Mary, I don't even want the damn sweater anymore and it looks great on you—just take it and don't make such a federal case out of it. You don't have to give me your firstborn.*

"Okay, I'll go." She relented. If she didn't sit down and get some nourishment to balance her blood sugar soon, this was all going to overwhelm her. "But I owe you for it."

"Pay me with a story," he said. "The whole story of what happened to you. Not to mention the fact that we need to figure out—" He stopped and touched her arm, then drew back. "Never mind, we'll worry about that later."

"Worry about it?" She felt the blood drain from her face. "What?"

He hesitated, then said, "At some point we need to find out who's buried in your grave."

Two hours later, over fifth and sixth cups of coffee, Drew had heard the entire story of Laura's past year. She didn't remember who had beaten her or what had led to the accident with her car. She also didn't remember where she'd been going in the car before it had all happened. All she did know was that she'd been found near a rest stop on I-95, apparently just twenty miles away from where someone else had crashed in her car.

Twenty miles away from where Drew stood, dying himself, in a dreary coroner's office, wondering how he was ever going to go on without her. Wondering how he was going to tell Samantha, and if she was capable of understanding at all.

Laura had been taken to a local hospital, where they'd treated her physical wounds. They'd run her fingerprints and come up with nothing, and without answers from her about her identity, the authorities had been forced to turn her case over to social services.

Social services had, in turn, taken her to a halfway house for women, called Sisters Anonymous. There, she had completed her physical recovery and eventually worked there and began her new life as Mary Shepherd.

She'd been there for more than a year, trying to forge a new identity—with her family so nearby, needing her, trying so hard to get along without her.

She'd fought to create a life, while a grave two hundred and fifty miles away had her name on it.

His thoughts returned to the body in the grave. The one he had identified as best he could, at the urging of impatient officials, eager to get on with business. The only recognizable aspect was that it was a woman's body. Naturally they had assumed...

He shook his head grimly. She was right. It was a stupid assumption. Now they'd have to exhume that body and try and figure out, more than a year later, who it was.

And why.

But right now none of it mattered. Right now the only thing he was sure of was that he had Laura back and they had to find a way to rebuild their marriage, to build a whole new future and get past the year they'd lost.

"So where's your stuff?" he asked, and took a sip of his water. "We've got to get you back home."

She froze. Fear he'd never seen in those eyes before made them wide. "Home?"

"Yeah." He tried to sound encouraging but the fear was unsettling. "You are planning on coming home with me now, aren't you?"

"I—I—no. I hadn't even begun to think about that yet. This is all so unexpected."

Dread nestled in the pit of his stomach. She didn't want to come home? "You must have realized someday you'd remember your first twenty-eight years and want to return to them."

"I'm twenty-nine?" Her question, and the soft surprise in her voice, caught him off guard.

"Yes. As of the twenty-first of April."

Something had changed in her expression, making him feel protective. "I had finally accepted the fact that I *wouldn't* ever regain those years. However many there were." She gave a wry smile.

"You can have them back, and more. Just come home."

She brushed her hand across her forehead, lifting her hair and letting it drop back into place. "I've got a life now, a new life, working at the shelter. I can't just abandon it."

He frowned. "You can't?"

She raised an eyebrow. "Can I?"

"Yes. Of course." His voice was short with frustration. "Your life is with me, with our daughter."

"But—that's not my life. I mean, you've told me it is, but that seems like someone else's." She shook her head and raised a hand that trembled to her eyes. "I can't just take her place, even if she's...me."

He reached his hand across the table and, watching him steadily, she slipped her hand into it. He remembered with absolute clarity the feel of it, the size and shape and the exact pressure against his. He put his other hand on top of hers and rubbed his thumb gently across her knuckles. "You *are* her, luckily for all of us," he told her. He wanted to raise her hand to his lips but something told him she wasn't ready for even that much intimacy. "This is *your* life."

"So you say."

She didn't trust him. A year had passed and taken

with it all of her memory, and she *still* didn't trust him. Hell, she didn't even *know* him and she didn't trust him. It had been the frustration of his life.

But over the last year or so he'd realized something about that frustration, and about her trust. His impatience had done nothing to make the situation better—it hadn't made him feel any better and it definitely hadn't made her trust him any more. He'd wondered, a million times, if a small investment of time might have made the difference.

Instead, he'd lost patience with her, driven her away, quite possibly to her death. How many times had he sworn that if he only had it to do over again, things would be different.

Now he did.

Swallowing the old habit of intolerance, he repeated the words he'd said so many times in the past. Words he'd once grown sick of saying, came out with renewed energy. "Laura, I've never lied to you."

She gave a wan smile. "That's what you'd say if you were lying, isn't it?"

He lost his breath. Even his heartbeat seemed to cease.

"What is it? What did I say?" she asked, looking alarmed at his expression.

He cocked his head. "You said that's what I'd say if I were lying to you."

"I was kidding."

He nodded slowly. "You've said it to me a million times before. Exactly the way you did just now. It got to be sort of a running joke with us." He smiled. They may have been the same old words, but they didn't have the same old ring. The truth suddenly felt fresh, and Drew felt an optimism unlike anything he'd ever felt before. This was his second chance to treat her, and those insecurities of hers, with the care he'd so often regretted not giving in the past.

Laura frowned, uncomprehending; then her expression cleared. "Are you saying you think I'm pretending not to remember?"

"No, I didn't say that." Though the idea hadn't entirely left him, it had been squashed by the revelation that he suddenly had the chance to be the man he always should have been. "I think the memories are all in there, close to the surface. Close enough for you to access them without realizing it." *Close enough to have a tremendous impact on our future, either for better or worse.*

"And close enough to have drawn me back to Nantucket," she agreed, and her expression softened, became almost dreamy.

"To your family." He wanted to reach for her, to touch her face, her skin, her hair, to assure himself that she was real. "I want you to come home."

Then something terrible occurred to him. What sort of impact would it make on Samantha to have a mother who didn't remember her?

"What about Samantha?" she asked, as if reading his mind. She'd always had a disturbing knack for that. "She can't see me like—like this."

He wanted to argue, to reassure her and persuade her to come home, but he knew she was right. "You're probably right."

"So..." She shrugged.

"I'll speak with the school psychologist tomorrow and find out the best way to handle this."

Laura closed her eyes tightly, and when she looked

back at him they were bright with unshed tears. "This is so hard."

"It *is* hard," he agreed. "Things like this don't happen outside of books and movies, but—" he splayed his hands "—here we are. As far as I'm concerned, it's a miracle. The best thing that ever happened to me. I thought you were dead but you're *alive*. How many people get that kind of second chance?"

"Second chance," she mused. "Funny, it feels more like a first chance."

He nodded. He would have given anything to make it easier for her but that was impossible. The only thing that would make it easier would be to go back and erase the past. "If we're going to move forward, we're going to have to stop dwelling on how weird this is, and take it the way we're getting it, one moment at a time."

She pressed her lips together and nodded. "It's hard to contemplate the future when you can't even begin to comprehend the present."

There was nothing fragile about the strong woman before him, yet Drew wanted to take her into his arms and protect her from the hellish darkness in her mind. "You'll probably start to remember things when you see home. Seems like the sooner the better."

"I can't do that. I know I lived there before, but I can't get around the fact that I'm not that person anymore, and I can't just step into her life as if nothing ever happened. I'm not ready to just move in with you. You have to respect that."

He laughed softly.

"What's funny?"

"It's not the first time you've said that, either. The

part about not being ready to live with me, and me having to respect that, I mean.'' His arms ached to throw the table aside and pull her against him, but he resisted. ''In fact, I think those were your exact words before we were married.''

''Then I'm one smart woman,'' she said with a trace of humor in her eyes. ''If repetitive.''

''Always were. Smart, I mean. And somewhat repetitive, now that I think about it.'' He smiled. ''But I didn't mean to push you. I was suggesting you come *see* the place, see if it sparks anything or brings anything back to you.''

''Oh.'' She laughed. ''That probably is a good idea, then.''

He signaled the waiter for the check and took a gold credit card out of his wallet. ''So where are you staying?'' He hated the words, even though he had to say them, because it sounded like he was giving credence to the idea that she might not come back home.

''Starbuck House,'' she answered. ''Where do you live?''

''Just a couple miles from there.'' He resisted the thought that she already knew that, and looked at his watch. ''Sam goes to bed in about an hour. How about I go home and tuck her in and you come over and case the joint while she's asleep? That'll be less pressure for you and for her, and it might trigger a memory or two.'' *Then it will all come back to you, everything will be normal and we can start to put the pieces of our lives back together.*

''This is a lot all at once.'' She pursed her lips and thought. She didn't remember having a child, but over the past year she'd felt a longing for one. She didn't want to ruin this by scaring the child. She had to be careful. So careful. "Maybe we should try it in the morning instead. Will she be at school then?"

Drew nodded, reluctantly. "From eight to one. I have a baby-sitter, currently on overtime, who takes care of her during the day. She could take her on some sort of excursion tomorrow if we need to buy some extra time before you meet her."

"I *want* to meet her, you know." Her voice was soft. "More than anything. But I don't want to frighten her. I don't have any idea how I'm going to react to all of this, and kids can see right through you, no matter how good an act you put on."

"You're right. You were always better with her than I was. Before I became Mr. Mom anyway."

"Was I?"

He nodded. "It's that intuition or something." Laura's eyes brightened when he said that, in that way they always did when she was pleased. Or aroused. The pit of his stomach tightened and his heart sped up. This was not the time to be thinking about Laura aroused. "I can't believe I'm having this conversation. With *you*. Laura, I'm so glad you're back."

She looked into his eyes. "I think..." She sighed. "Thanks."

He eyed her for a second, then scribbled the address on a napkin and handed it to her with a ten-dollar bill. "This is the address. Any cabdriver will be able to find it, no problem."

She took the napkin from him but not the money. "Eight o'clock?"

They stood up.

"I'll be waiting," he said as they walked toward the door. He'd take the week off, he decided. More, if necessary. When they got outside, he stopped. "Laura."

She kept walking.

"Laura," he said a little louder.

"Oh!" She stopped and turned around. "That's going to take a while to get used to."

The golden twilight made her skin tawny, and her eyes a bright vivid blue. Her hair gleamed, deep and rich. Drew's breath caught in his throat and he tried to swallow a memory. They used to make love on long summer days, with the afternoon sun pouring through the window and drenching them both in amber. This was a poignant glimpse of that shared past.

He could barely find his voice. "Laura" was all he managed to say.

A smile curled the side of her mouth. "Yes?"

The hell with right and wrong, he thought. In one swift, unstoppable movement, he pulled her into an embrace.

She didn't resist.

The relief of having her in his arms again was like a drug. Her body was soft and pliant. Thinner than before, but still painfully familiar.

"I don't want to let you go," he murmured against her hair. It smelled fruity, and that surprised him. She was using a different shampoo. Unfamiliar. It made sense yet it was disconcerting. "Now that I've seen you again, I don't want to let you out of my sight. I'm afraid you'll disappear again, or this will all turn out to be a dream."

"It's no dream," she said against his shoulder. He felt her hands sweep gingerly across his back before resting there. She turned her face and rested it against his chest. He felt her relax in his arms. "It's been a long time for me, too."

Only, I have some resolution now, he thought. *You, on the other hand, have to believe all of this on my word. That's the sort of faith you always had trouble with.* He squeezed tighter. "I promise you can trust me," he said in answer to his own thoughts. "You're not going to get hurt."

She pulled back, looking surprised. "I'm not worried about my getting hurt. I'm worried about hurting everyone else, letting you all down."

He chuckled softly. "Sweetheart, you've just risen from the dead. What could you possibly do to let anyone down at this point?"

"I might never remember you."

"I don't believe that."

"It's been over a year with nothing. It's hard for me to believe it's ever going to come back."

He refused to acknowledge the possibility that she might be right. "In that year you've never seen your home or your family or any of the people and places that meant so much to you. Something is bound to trigger your memory and it'll all come back to you."

Her blue eyes dimmed. He recognized an inner wince. "I don't think it works that way."

He smiled.

"What?" she asked. "I wasn't trying to be funny."

"You weren't trying to be Laura Bennett, either, but you did it. You always expect the worst in almost every situation. You always said that was the best way to avoid disappointment but it's not true."

She looked down. "Is that so?"

"You know it's so." He laughed. "That's why you're not looking at me."

She scoffed and looked him directly in the eye, but not before he continued. "Now you'll look at me square on—ah, there you go—to prove to me that you *can* look me in the eye." Before she could speak, he held up a hand and said, "Don't deny it."

Her cheeks flushed. "What did you do, create me?"

"No," he said softly, brushing a finger across her pink cheek. "No, I loved you."

The expression in her eyes softened then, but she didn't look away.

They stood facing each other, eyes locked, but without challenge.

Drew thought he could see the woman he knew deep, deep in her eyes. But there was another woman there now, too. A strong, independent, even *feisty* woman, who had no history. This woman who had never loved a man, who had never had children. A woman who wasn't worn down to the bone by the day-to-day grind of being a housewife in a tiny town surrounded by water.

"Look," he said at last. "Let's do this without pressure or expectation. Maybe coming home will trigger your memory and maybe it won't. If it doesn't, I want to get to know you again. I want *you* to get to know *me*." It was on the tip of his tongue to mention her being a mother to Sam, but he held back, not wanting to add any more pressure on her. "Let's just see what happens and make decisions later, okay?"

She had tears in her eyes. "You were—are—kind. You're a...a good man. I'm not saying this well. It's just that most women don't have such caring husbands.''

He smiled, but felt it fall quickly. She said that *now,* but what would happen when she got her memory back and knew all the troubles they'd had before the accident?

It was all too possible that those feelings would come back to her as fresh as if it had all happened yesterday, rather than mellowed by the months of separation they'd had to endure. He wasn't even sure sitting with it all that time would mellow her—eight years hadn't.

The thought was too horrible to contemplate, but it slithered into his mind like a snake pushing through the crevice of a rock.

What if she regained her memory and remembered their impending divorce?

Chapter Four

Laura spent the night in room 4B of Starbuck House pacing. The day's events were too much to comprehend. She'd expected she would feel relieved to learn who she was, but she didn't. All she had were facts and explanations; the memories hadn't come crashing back the way they always did on the TV movie-of-the-week, so she ended up with more questions than ever.

But at least she was finally learning the truth about herself, her life. It seemed like there should have been some satisfaction in that fact, but there wasn't. On the other hand, maybe it was easier to live in the anonymity she'd become accustomed to, rather than trying to figure out who she was and what—and who—she was responsible for.

She'd thought that she'd be able to make some sense of it all when she was alone, but instead she found she was more adrift than before. The suffocating feeling she had attributed to Drew's close proximity to her at Arno's was actually worse in his absence.

He wasn't closing in on her, her life was. Like an invisible net, letting everything around her escape. Everything but her. Suddenly Mary Shepherd's life seemed like a faraway dream, and this—Laura—a heavy reality.

The phone rang by her bedside. She rushed to pick it up. "Hello?"

"Hi, Mar, it's me." It was Nella Laraby, the director of Sisters Anonymous. "Got some of those answers you were looking for."

"Already?" Laura glanced at the clock. She'd only placed the call to Nella two and a half hours ago, as soon as she'd left Drew.

"I've got some connections on the force." Nella liked to talk like that—"the force" was the Wayne County Police Department, which had well under fifty employees, and her "connections" consisted primarily of a mousy clerk who had come to Sisters Anonymous seventeen years before. But most of the police force were friends of Nella's, and of Sisters Anonymous. "All I had to do was mention your name and the guys were jumping."

Laura switched the receiver from one hand to the other. "And what did they find out?"

"Your guy checks out."

She swallowed. "Meaning...?" she asked, even though she knew what it meant.

"Meaning you apparently are Laura Bennett. The photos that came over the fax certainly looked like you. She was reported DOA at Litchfield Memorial Hospital in February last year, but the ID was circumstantial to say the least."

Laura's chest tightened. She was almost afraid of her next question. "Anything there about the history of Laura and Drew Bennett?"

"Nothing negative." Nella's voice was crisp but triumphant. "No 911 calls, no history of domestic squabbles. All reports were that he was devastated by his wife's loss. At least he acted that way," she added, somewhat coarsely.

Laura let out a long breath. "So it's all true, then. He's my...he's my husband."

"As far as we can tell," Nella agreed across the wire. "But that's no reason to rush things. You don't want to dive headlong into an unfamiliar or uncomfortable situation."

Laura shook her head, even though Nella couldn't see her. One thing her meeting with Drew had *not* been was uncomfortable. "I have to stay and see this through now, Nella. At least for a while. I don't think Drew poses any sort of threat to me or my well-being."

"Your instincts have always been excellent, Mary—I mean Laura. But don't let that lull you into a false sense of security. Until you really know this man, not on paper but in person, you must be cautious."

"I will be."

"And don't forget the most important thing."

After an expectant silence, Laura asked, "What's that?"

"You're not just responsible for yourself anymore." Nella paused dramatically. "From now on you have a little one to consider."

From now on you have a little one to consider. For as long as she could remember, Laura had never taken that consideration before. Suddenly, with virtually no maternal experience, she had to somehow find a way to act in the best interest of her child.

Nella went on to volunteer to come to Nantucket in a heartbeat if Laura needed her for anything at all. She also insisted on at least finding the name of a good counselor in the area, in case Laura needed one. Laura thanked her and replaced the receiver, after promising to keep in close touch. This was something she had to work through alone.

So Drew Bennett was telling the truth. She was relieved—no, that was an understatement—she was glad to hear it. Now she could allow herself at least a few of the indulgent fantasies she'd been conjuring about him. Just a few. If there was one thing her year at Sisters Anonymous had taught her, it was to take things slowly.

No matter how much she might want to rush certain things.

She pictured Drew Bennett in her mind's eye. Even though she'd only just met him, not a detail was missing—from the dark chestnut eyes to the almost-imperceptible bump in his nose. She liked his nose. It looked like it had been broken once, a long time ago. She'd seen enough of that at the shelter to recognize it. Interesting. Of course, it could have come from an accident or something, not in a fight as one immediately assumed.

Then there was the curve of his mouth, the one small physical detail that had intrigued her the most. One corner tilted ever so slightly upward, like the mouth of a man who smiled often and easily. His lips weren't overly full but they also weren't the tight, hard lines that came from years of anger. They were, she realized, just right.

The few seconds that she'd been able to feel them on hers had done nothing to sate her curiosity. In fact, it had only made things worse.

She wondered what it would be like to really kiss those lips, to drown in deep, wet kisses, then realized with a small laugh that she already knew. She knew that and much more undoubtedly. She sat down on the corner of the bed and caught her reflection in the mirror opposite. Where else had his lips touched her? Had he kissed her neck? Her skin tingled at the thought. Was he the sort to whisper sweet nothings and trail kisses down her back? Was he a hungry lover, or a shy one?

Somewhere, locked behind some iron door in her mind, were the answers to those questions and more. She wished she could take at least a peek at them. If only to satisfy some of this building curiosity about Drew.

She stood up and walked to the window. The moon was almost full. Somewhere in the back of her mind she remembered that it always appeared full the night before it actually was. The difference was in the brilliance of the light. Tonight it was like a silver dollar resting on deep purple velvet. Filmy clouds scudded across its surface and disappeared into the Milky Way.

She leaned against the windowsill and rested her forehead on the cool glass. On the street below, trees and parking meters cast long shadows from the streetlights. She had to stop wondering who Drew Bennett was, and start wondering who Laura Bennett was.

That was easier said than done. Just when she'd

finally accepted the fact that she had no one, and would never have the part of her life that was missing, it had hit her full in the face. It was like a miracle.

No one ever said miracles weren't scary.

Laura pushed away from the windowsill and walked across the room to where her suitcase was. Absently she leafed through the clothes and found the pretty flannel nightgown she'd splurged on for the trip. Everyone said to expect warm days but chilly nights up north. She pulled her shirt off and unhooked her bra, and the thought of Drew came back to her.

Had those hands danced across this very rib cage? Had she lain next to that lean, strong body night after night for eight years before the accident? Had those arms enfolded her in times of need and passion? Did she know what it felt like to run her fingers slowly through his glossy dark hair as they lay side by side in the dark?

She must.

She unsnapped her jeans and slipped out of them, trying to dismiss further thoughts of intimacy with Drew. It was stupid—the last thing she needed to think about right now. Her curiosity about carnal knowledge of this man, whether he was her husband or not, wasn't her highest priority.

Her highest priority was the welfare of her daughter. She had a daughter. How long was it going to take to get used to that idea? The pain of knowing that Samantha was out there, a little girl separated from her mother, was too great to contemplate. But the alternative was to not think about her at all, and that was even more difficult.

So why are you here alone instead of at your home

with your husband and child? a nagging voice inside her asked.

"Because," she answered, as if speaking to another person in the room, "I'm terrified that when I see her my whole life will come crashing down on me and I'll have a nervous breakdown on the spot, right there in front of her. Besides, we have to wait and see how the school psychologist says to handle it." *So there,* she added silently to her nagging conscience.

She slipped the nightgown over her head and pulled back the bed sheets. *It can wait until tomorrow,* she told herself. *That's not so long, not after fifteen months. And at least this way I'll be able to get used to being at the house before she sees me. And before I see her.* She sat heavily and looked at the clock on the bedside table: 10:45 p.m.

It had been fifteen long months. But in nine hours, Mary Shepherd would disappear forever and Laura Bennett would be going home.

Her first thought when the cab pulled up outside the whitewashed clapboard house the next morning was that the house looked like something from a Norman Rockwell painting. The white fence surrounding the property had been painted recently. Pansies lined the drive, and there was a trellis against the garage with pink baby roses winding around its white wooden slats.

She walked slowly up the walk, hearing the hum of the taxicab driving away. The front door opened before she got to it and Drew stood before her, even more handsome than she'd remembered from the day before. *He looks like a movie star,* she thought absently. *How did I luck into a guy that looks like that?*

She sighed. These and many other questions would have to be answered in time.

"Hi," he said, running a hand across his brow. Laura noticed he had shadows under his eyes, as if he hadn't slept. He gave a flicker of a smile. "Welcome home."

Thunder rumbled through her chest. "Thanks." *None of this is familiar—not the house, not the street, not the trellis, nothing.* Yet the hum within her increased with every step she took.

"You...don't recognize the house." It was a statement, not a question.

"Am I that transparent?" Laura asked.

"I've seen that look on your face before." His disappointment was obvious.

"Of course. That I-don't-remember-my-home look? Do I have a history of amnesia?" She smiled but inside she ached. It was disconcerting to be with someone who knew so much more about her than she herself did.

"None." He reconsidered. "None that you ever told me about."

Her eyes widened. "How long have you known me?"

He smiled. "Since you were eighteen."

"Ah." She relaxed some. "So...probably not."

"I don't think so." He stepped aside, sweeping his arm toward the open door. "Are you ready to come in?"

She took a breath. "About as ready as I'll be today." She let the breath out and walked through the doorway. *Why do I feel like I should be wearing a crash helmet?*

If she'd expected to feel a bolt of recognition, she

was disappointed. Instead, it felt like walking into any house in any neighborhood in the world. She saw everything from a detached point of view. The knotty pine floors and wainscoting were charming but unfamiliar, the overstuffed sofa faced a cavernous stone fireplace like none she'd ever seen before. The braided rug was worn, the colors softened to pastel probably from years of feet upon it, but she didn't remember it.

Her heart sank a few notches. "Why did I think this was going to be easy?"

Drew came up behind her. "You *hoped* it would be easy. So did I. But it was no simple matter for you to die, so naturally it's not going to be a simple matter for you to come back to life."

She rubbed her hands across the gooseflesh on her arms. "That sounds so creepy."

"Sorry." He gave a sort of embarrassed smile, and a moment of awkward silence passed before he said, "I was reading up on the rate of recovery from amnesia and it's almost never an instantaneous thing. It's a long road and it takes a lot of little steps to get there. It's going to take a lot of patience."

He'd been reading up on her condition? Laura found the idea strangely touching. "Yes, of course you're right."

He gave a brief, devastating smile. "But you're not in this alone," he said in a soft voice. "You have me. And I'm going to do everything I can to help you."

Laura felt herself leaning toward him, and pulled back. "Like maybe a good conk on the head?" she tried to joke. "It always works in cartoons."

"Yeah, well, I don't want to be cliché but life is not a cartoon."

"As they say." She smiled.

He looked deep into her eyes. "As they say."

"They also say you can't go home again." The words came out in an emotional rush.

He ran his knuckle along her jawline, then cupped her cheek with his hand. "You can if you want to."

She lifted her hand to his. "I want..." She hesitated, then sighed and met his eyes directly. "I *want* to want to, if that makes any sense. But this still doesn't feel like my—" She stopped. Something on the mantelpiece caught her eye. "What's that?"

He dropped his hand and turned to look in that direction. "What? What are you looking at?"

She walked slowly toward the fireplace. Everything seemed still. "This." When she got to the mantel, she reached for a painted wooden horse, about five inches tall. There was a momentary shock of familiarity when she took it in her hand. Something about the smooth lacquer of the paint, and the subtle ridges in the wood from hand carving. The horse was orange with colorful flowers painted on it. She gripped it, straining to remember, but felt the recognition slip away like a raft on a lake, and soon it was too distant to see.

"Your grandfather got that ages ago in Mexico. I think you had it your whole life. You said it brought good luck. It's been right there on the mantel ever since we moved in."

She examined the horse, now more objectively. A lot of people might have thought it was tacky but she didn't. Even though the momentary spark was past, she found the piece appealing.

"You felt something?" Drew asked. "A little something?"

She considered, and nodded slowly. "A little. Maybe." She shrugged apologetically. "I'm not sure."

"It'll come." He jerked his hand toward the kitchen. "You want some tea or something?"

"No, thanks. I think I'll just browse some." Laura walked across the room to where a collection of photos sat on a piano. "Do you play?" she asked Drew.

"No, you do. Or you did. Before."

She looked down at her hands, then at the piano keys. Nothing came to her. That was someone else. She ran her fingers across the walnut lid of the piano, then, startled, took a photo in her hand. "This guy." She held up the picture for him to see. "Who is he?"

Drew raised his eyebrows. "You remember him?"

"Yes, from yesterday. He followed me through town. I figured he was some sort of lunatic."

Drew laughed, a hearty, rich laugh. "That's Vince. He was the best man at our wedding."

"I seriously doubt it."

He laughed again. It was a good sound. "Come to think of it, he always did sort of get on your nerves."

"Well, then, not everything's changed. That's comforting." She picked up another picture, this one of a woman with short blond hair, holding in her arms the little girl Laura now knew was her daughter. The woman was very pretty.

A twinge buzzed through Laura's chest.

It hadn't really occurred to her that Drew might have gotten involved with someone else in the months since her "death." Of course he had every right to, but... She'd just assumed he hadn't. Stupid. She'd only known him for a day, she didn't know anything about him.

Maybe he was engaged to this woman. Good Lord, maybe even married, with kids... No, surely he would have mentioned *that*.

Unless he thought it would be too upsetting for her.

She held the picture up for Drew. "And who's this?" She didn't want to hear the answer.

"That's Mindy."

"Mindy."

He cocked his head and smiled. "My secretary."

"Aha." Laura looked back at the picture. No wonder she hadn't entirely trusted him, if his office was staffed with women who looked like Mindy. "Has she always gotten on my nerves, too?"

"No." Drew took a few steps toward her and held her gaze with the hot intensity of his. "Apparently that's new."

But it didn't feel new; it felt old. It felt like someone else's feelings, not her own. "I didn't mean that." Her protest sounded a little hollow, even to her own ears. She left the pictures and walked casually to the desk, trailing her finger along the corner of the wood. There were papers scattered across it, but the mess was oddly charming. "I'm merely trying to orient myself."

His eyes were filled with humor. "Of course."

"I am!" But she had to laugh. She wasn't fooling either one of them. She picked up a pile of business cards and started to leaf through casually. "Do you mind?"

"Not at all. Are you looking for an architect?"

She looked back at the cards and saw that they were all, indeed, architects and contractors—Vincent Reese, William Henderson. She flipped across them until she came to one with a photo on it. Laura's hand started to shake. It was a photo of a woman with very pale hair and eyes. *Gena Finley.* She dropped the card. "Oh, I'm sorry."

"It's okay." Drew reached for the card at the same time and their fingertips touched. "Hey, you're shaking."

Laura's first thought was that she'd had too much coffee, but something inside told her it wasn't caffeine. Was it the woman in the picture? Or someone she reminded Laura of? "Who is Gena Finley?" She searched his eyes for some reaction but was struck only by the control she saw there.

"Gena Finley used to work for my firm. She was in the Boston office." He stopped, but it seemed abrupt.

"She used to work there? What happened to her?"

He shrugged. "She quit. I don't know what happened to her after that."

Laura frowned. "Does she live here?"

"On Nantucket?" He shook his head. "No. I don't even think she lives in Boston anymore. In fact, there were rumors that she just disappeared. Now that I think of it—" he lowered his voice in a mock conspiratorial way "—it was right around the time *you* disappeared." He lowered his voice. "What did you do with her, Laura?"

She shook her head and smiled. "Point taken. Was I a particularly jealous wife?"

His answer was immediate. "Oh, yeah. You had a real problem with that. Especially at the end, you were..." He didn't finish but his eyes flicked to the card in her hand. Obviously he wanted to change the subject.

She raised an eyebrow, feeling protective of the self

she didn't know. "Did I ever have reason to be jealous?"

"Never." He shook his head, then looked at the papers on the desk behind her. "Not even the slightest. But you *always* had trouble believing that."

"Hmm. Do you think that might be because you have trouble saying it?"

"I don't have any trouble saying it."

"The words came out fine." Nella's voice came back to her. *Until you really know this man, not on paper but in person, you must be cautious.* She looked at him evenly. "But you didn't look me in the eye."

His expression darkened. "I've never been much good at having to defend myself against your crazy accusations."

She raised her eyebrows. "Did you always call them crazy?"

"Not always." There was a barely perceptible edge to his voice. "I was patient for the first six or seven years. *Then* I began to feel like *maybe* you didn't trust me, even though I hadn't done anything to deserve that lack of trust. Maybe I'm weird, but that bugged me."

"And I suppose you were a perfect angel."

He froze and looked into her eyes. "I didn't say that."

"Well, so far I've heard all about *my* mistakes and shortcomings, but nothing about yours."

"Maybe I didn't have any?" He tried to laugh.

"No offense, but I can't believe that."

"Well, then, maybe I made so many mistakes and had so many shortcomings that I don't want to remind you of them." He tried to make it sound like a joke, but something in his eyes told her that this was probably much closer to the truth. At least from his point of view.

"There's something about us that you're trying not to tell me." It was a statement and she was certain she was right. What she hadn't recognized at first, she now saw was a trace of guilt in his eyes. It had been there ever since they'd first spoken. Why?

After a long hesitation he said, "I worked a lot. Always hated the word *workaholic*, but too many people have called me that to discount it completely. It caused...tension between us. You wanted me to spend more time at home, with you and with Sam."

"That doesn't sound unreasonable."

He grimaced. "It wasn't unreasonable—I wanted that, too. It's just that back then I had to work so hard to get the business off the ground so we could keep our home. We had some lean days in the beginning."

Laura sighed. It was hard to defend a woman she didn't know, even if it *was* herself. Maybe she *had* been some sort of shrew of a wife, or neurotic, or maybe she'd been a terrible mother. Was he trying to protect her from that knowledge?

Was he trying to protect Sam from it?

The thought was horrifying. She had to steer away from it. "Okay, let's call a truce. We can continue this later, when I know you better."

"Let's not continue it at all." He stepped up to her and put his hands on both her shoulders. "One thing this mess has done for us is erase the swamp of habits we'd formed—habits of not trusting, not taking the time to understand each other, not trying." He hesitated. "Not compromising."

"Not compromising?" she repeated. "Not try-ing?" She bit down on her lower lip. What was behind those words? "There it is again. I keep getting the feeling that there are a lot of things you don't want to tell me about."

"Now you're psychic?"

She wasn't going to be deflected by his flippancy. "You don't need to protect me."

"I know." But he didn't sound as if he believed it.

She had to ask, even though she wasn't sure she wanted the answer. "Drew, did we have marital problems?"

A beat passed, then he shrugged. "Everyone has some."

She searched his face. Again he was being flip, almost too casual. "No, I mean significant ones. I noticed—I couldn't help but notice, I mean, that there are no pictures of me around here." She gestured toward the sideboard where all the other photos were. "It's not vanity, you understand. That just seems…I don't know, odd."

He looked down for a long moment before looking back at her. "After you…after I *thought* you died, it was just so…hard." He shook his head and shrugged. "And Sam couldn't let go, either. A counselor suggested that I put the pictures away for a while."

She nodded. "I can understand that. But there are other things, things you said. Was our marriage in trouble?"

He moved his hands to cup her face. "I never stopped loving you," he said quietly. He ran his thumbs across her temples, and tangled his fingers in her hair. He leaned slightly toward her. Their lips were almost within kissing distance. Almost, but not quite. "You have to believe that, if nothing else. I *never* stopped loving you."

Suddenly she felt weak. She *wanted* to believe him, but something in her made her ask, "But did I stop loving you?"

His gaze deepened. "No." Laura thought she saw something in it. Regret? Worry? She couldn't tell. "I don't think so."

His voice—she didn't know if it was the timbre or the sincerity of his words—went right to her heart. At that moment she wanted to be closer to him. She knew she shouldn't but she wanted to comfort him, to smooth the worry lines from his face, to kiss him until there was no trace of regret in his eyes.

Was this feeling new? Or was it the remnants of love that she could feel but not remember?

Her chest tingled. His breath was hot against her lips, her chin, her cheeks. His eyes—those piercing eyes—were so close, she could swear he could see right into her.

An instinct kicked in, an instinct she didn't know she had, and she tilted her head and parted her lips slightly. "Then I'll have to believe you," she said in a too-breathy voice. *Please kiss me*, she thought irrationally. *Please, please kiss me.*

"You're not known for your faith in me."

"You have all my faith now." She looked up at him. If she took one step closer she'd be pressed right against him.

He drew in a long breath, holding her gaze with his own. She saw him swallow, then swallow again. His hand moved slowly toward her face but he stopped. He held her gaze for another long moment, then stepped back from her. His hands trailed slowly across her shoulders and down her arms, burning a path in their wake. He took her hands in his. "We shouldn't do that."

"Do what?" she asked, a little flustered.

"Kiss."

Her face burned and she was positive it was a tell-tale crimson. "Who said anything about kissing?"

"Not that I don't want to," he continued. "Believe me, I do. There are a *lot* of things I'd like to do with you, but I think we really have to take this slow."

Who have you been talking to? she asked silently. A picture of Mindy came to mind and doused what was left of her desire with cold water. "Not that I wanted to kiss you," she tried to scoff, "but where are you getting your information on what we can and cannot do?"

"I told you, I've been reading. It's very important not to overstimulate the patient."

"'The patient,'" she repeated. "Meaning me?"

He grinned. "Patience isn't something I'd normally attribute to you, but yes, meaning you."

She attempted a laugh. "It's been at least fifteen months—I don't think there's any such thing as over-stimulation at this point."

The grin widened devilishly. "You really don't remember being with me, do you? You'd be surprised."

"That's quite an ego you have, Mr. Bennett."

He studied her for a moment, then laughed. "I was joking. Come on, Laura. You don't need to get snippy. I wanted it, too, but I don't want to make things worse for you."

"Thanks."

"So," he continued, "ready to see the rest of the castle?"

She nodded. "If you don't think I'll be overstimulated by it."

He smiled and let go of her hands. "How about the bedroom?"

She jerked her head up.

"I didn't mean—" He laughed. "You decorated it yourself. Sam's room, too. I thought you might like to see it, see if it brings anything back to you."

"Of course," she murmured.

He led the way up the stairs and down a long hallway. The floors were knotty pine here, too, but covered with Oriental carpet runners. She stopped every once in a while to scrutinize a picture on the wall, or the view out of a window. Nothing.

Sam's room was a delicate peach color, with white furniture, including a white canopy bed with lace trimmings. There was a large bookshelf filled with thin-spined colorful books. Laura walked over to it and read some of the titles. *"Goodnight Moon. Guess How Much I Love You. Linnea in Monet's Garden."* She turned to Drew. "I guess Sam's a pretty big bookworm."

"She got that from you."

Her heart warmed, flushing her cheeks. "Really?"

"You liked to read to her." He glanced down, and when he met her eyes again his expression was heavy with melancholy. "You did it every night."

Laura's heart constricted. She pictured herself on that frilly bed, reading fairy tales and *Winnie-the-Pooh* to her little girl. Was it her imagination or was the picture in her head a memory? A playback of something that had really happened. She didn't know. "I'd still like that," she said in a choked voice.

She heard the floor creak as he took a step toward

her, then felt Drew's warm hand on her shoulder. "You can still do that," Drew said softly in her ear. "You lost a year, but you didn't lose her whole childhood."

Laura nodded, unable to find her voice.

"How would you like to see your reading room?" Drew asked, slipping his hand into hers and giving a tug. "Come on, you're going to love this."

She followed him to the room next door. It was a large bedroom, converted into a personal library. Apart from a large stone fireplace on the left, the walls were lined with dark wood shelves that stretched from floor to ceiling. The hardwood floors matched the shelves and had two dark cranberry-colored braided rugs on them. A blue-and-white daybed with puffy pillows faced the fireplace. A small table by the daybed held a Tiffany glass lamp and a shiny black old-fashioned telephone.

"This is incredible," Laura murmured. "How did I ever leave this room?"

Drew laughed.

She meandered along the walls, running her fingers along the spines of books, occasionally taking one out and examining it. There were old hardbound books, and recent paperbacks, all mixed together. It was glorious.

She walked back to where Drew leaned back on the daybed. "Who built this place?"

"We did. That is, I put the shelves in and you put the books in. There's not much more to it. This bed was your grandmother's, and you found that old telephone at a flea market." He chuckled. "We had a heck of a time wiring it to work but we did."

She looked at the phone, then went to it and took

a closer look. It was black and so glossy, she could see her reflection in it, except for a few old scuffs and scratches.

But when she picked up the heavy receiver, a shudder ran through her. Horror. No sooner did she have the feeling, than it was gone, leaving a disturbing unease behind. She set the receiver back and said, "Where are you taking me next?"

He eyed her suspiciously. "You don't want to look around in here anymore?"

She looked down at the phone. Something about it disturbed her. She felt like she didn't even want to be in the same room with it. "No. There's nothing here."

He followed her gaze to the phone and, as if on cue, it rang.

Her heart stopped. It wasn't a regular ring, but rather a high series of little bells, distinct in that one or two of them thudded dully rather than ringing. It rang again.

This time it brought something harshly to mind. It wasn't a memory—it was more of an idea with an inexplicable certainty. She *knew*.

Drew had been having an affair.

Chapter Five

The shrill, distinct ring continued.

"I'll let the machine get it," Drew said. "Laura?"

Blood drained from her face, leaving her cold and, she was sure, pale. The phone stopped and she took a breath. Drew was having an affair? Where did that come from? "I'm sorry, I was thinking about something...." She looked at him.

His brow creased with concern. "Maybe this is too much for you all at once."

"No, I'm okay. It's just the phone—it's...so loud." *So dreadfully familiar. So important. Why?* She swallowed. "It—it surprised me."

This seemed to relieve him. "You're sure that's all?"

She blinked. "Yes. Yes, I'm sure." If there was any truth to that wild suspicion, she would have to find the answer on her own.

But looking into those warm, dark eyes of his now, she found it difficult to believe he was trying to de-

ceive her. That was the trouble with charming men—
they always managed to make people *want* to believe
them. So the fact that she had *a feeling* that she could
trust him, didn't necessarily mean anything. "Where
to next?" she asked, forcing the speculation to the
back of her mind for the moment.

He gestured to the door with his hand. "I'll follow
you. Feel your way."

Again she looked into his eyes and saw nothing but
sincerity. So much, in fact, that it made her stomach
do a funny little flip. "Which way is your—our
room?"

He didn't answer but looked at her for a hard moment before leading the way out through the hall to
the door at the end. He stopped, and tapped his
knuckle against it. "This was our room. I haven't
changed anything since you've been gone."

"Except the shoes."

"What?"

"My shoes. You said you gave them away."

"Ah, yes. That's right—to charity." He gave a
small shrug. "Actually, we put away or gave away
pretty much all of your personal things—clothes, jewelry and whatnot. I'm sorry."

"That's okay with me. I don't think I'm going to
miss any of it."

"But the room still looks the same," he offered.
"I mean, it's not a living shrine or anything. I just
didn't want to change anything."

He hadn't tried to sweep her memory out of his
life. Laura warmed. "I think that's nice."

"Well, a lot of people think that's nuts, so I just
wanted to tell you in advance. Not that you'd necessarily notice one way or the other."

"True." She gave a brief smile, then looked back at the door, waiting for him to open it, like the unveiling of an oil masterpiece.

He turned the knob and pushed the door open.

Taking what felt like slow, measured steps, Laura moved toward it. There was the merest hint of a familiar scent in the air. *Bay rum* came suddenly into her mind. *I like it. I think I've always liked it.* With one more glance at Drew, she walked through the doorway.

The ceiling was white with dark brown exposed beams. Two of the walls had two windows each, and sunshine poured in. Laura walked in slowly, taking the atmosphere in with her eyes, ears and nose. There was a rocking chair in the corner, with what looked like a handmade quilt folded over it and a small walnut table to the left. There was a book on the table and Laura walked over and picked it up. An old battered copy of R.A. Dick's *The Ghost and Mrs. Muir*, with a paper clip poking out from one of the middle pages.

She gestured at him with the book. "Mine?"

He nodded. "You loved it. I hoped it might trigger something." There was an awkward pause. "I've only seen the TV show. You know, Charles Nelson Reilly."

She didn't know, but she nodded and put the book down.

The windows had no curtains but instead had fabric shades. She'd seen something like that in a catalog once—one of those fancy catalogs that the women at the shelter looked at with longing, but not with credit cards in hand.

Then there was the bed. It had a carved wooden

headboard, and a patchwork quilt on it. It was made up but not very neatly. She suspected he didn't usually bother with that at all, and almost laughed at the thought when her eyes fell on something next to the floor. Something that made her heart trip.

She squinted and took a few steps toward it. No, it couldn't be. She looked closer. It was half in the shadows under the bed and half out, but there was no mistaking what it was.

It was a woman's gold earring.

Drew noticed her whole body stiffen, saw her eyes narrow, then widen. Then she made what looked like an effort to compose herself. What was she staring at? He followed her gaze to the bed. The bed? Was that it? One thing Laura had never been nervous about in the past was the bed.

"What's the matter?" he asked her. He tried to sound solicitous but his confusion rang clearly in his voice.

She swallowed, and drew a short breath. "I thought I saw...something. So, are these really support beams or just for show?"

"Support." He frowned, still looking by the bed. "What? Was it the quilt or something?"

"Nothing. Forget it."

He shifted his weight and caught a sparkle on the floor by the bed. In four fast strides he was there, bending to pick up an earring from the floor. "Is this what you saw?"

She squinted to see it, but the squint was too exaggerated. She was going to deny it but it would be a lie. "What is it?" she asked, trying not to let on how much the possible implications bothered her.

He tossed the earring onto the bedside table, where it clattered softly for a moment. "That belongs to some chick I had over the other night."

Laura's eyes widened.

Surely she hadn't taken him seriously! "Laura, I was—"

"You don't have to explain."

"—kidding." He took her by the arms. "Really, it was just a joke."

"Funny."

He couldn't stifle a laugh. "It is if you know me."

She shrugged out of his grasp. "Well, I *don't* know you." Her voice was clipped. "That's the point."

He cocked his head. "Now, here's a Laura I recognize," he said matter-of-factly. "Totally unable to take a joke, however stupid, and suspicious that it means something more."

"I don't think it's unreasonable for me to wonder why *my husband* has a woman's earring next to his bed."

"No," he agreed, glad, for the moment, to see her feeling some attachment to him, even if it was possessive. "No, that's not unreasonable. What's unreasonable is the conclusion that you jump to before even asking. It's unreasonable that you won't believe the truth once you've made up your own version."

"I didn't do that."

"You've *always* done that—you decide in advance what something means and then you won't change your mind, no matter what I say."

She shifted her weight. "I don't hear you saying anything. At least not about the earring or the woman it belongs to."

Drew almost smiled. It was also like Laura to drop

fear in the face of a fight. Right now that seemed like a good thing. Spirit overcoming trepidation. "That's what you're concerned about?"

She held her ground. "Curious," she said, "more than concerned. I mean, I don't care what you do with your private life, but I *hate* being lied to, especially now."

"Whoa! Slow down a minute there. Who lied? Sam was playing with the earring. I think the baby-sitter gave it to her to play dress-up. Big deal."

"All right." She raised her chin in a self-protective way he recognized. "But you're pretty defensive for a guy with nothing to hide."

He counted to ten silently. "I'm defensive, Laura, because I'm so sick of *explaining* myself, or more specifically, the things you imagine about me."

"I'm sorry I can't remember for myself," she huffed. "You're the one who insisted on giving me the grand tour—"

"I'm not talking about your memory, I'm talking about trust! These suspicions are nothing more than paranoia. That's what they've always been. They have *nothing* to do with your amnesia."

It was her turn to get icy with him. "Look, I'm swimming in murky water at best and you're divvying out information like it's food rations in World War II."

"No, I'm not."

"Oh, you are, too," she said quickly. "It's obvious."

"I've told you as plainly as I can—there's no other woman."

That stopped her cold. "You haven't told me that." She looked at him curiously.

"I have. A million times."

She crossed her arms in front of her and shifted her weight. "When?" she challenged. "Can you think of one time since you met me, or rather one time *this year* when that particular subject has even come up?"

The realization hit him like the ceiling falling in on top of him. Here he was, complaining that she was continuing old habits of mistrust when he, himself, was continuing a running argument that had ceased fifteen months before.

Before he could speak, she said, "The man doth protest too much, methinks."

"Maybe you're right, but not because there's another woman. There isn't." He shook his head in frustration. "You see, it was like this before you disappeared. Questions about everything I did, everything I said, everyone I talked to. Then when I answered you didn't believe me. Now you don't know who you are, who *I* am or what our relationship was like, and you *still* don't seem to trust me."

"Are you sure about that?"

"No." He couldn't bring himself to ask her directly.

"Then maybe you could give me the benefit of the doubt. And I'll try to do the same for you."

Guilt nudged at his conscience. He still hadn't been totally honest with her. But what good would it do? None. "I hate the mistrust," he said. He'd never actually let it go at that before. In the past, he'd made the repeated mistake of fighting her over it, taking his stand in the opposite corner. He realized now that had only fanned the flames.

"I'm not acting on a history of mistrust right now, Drew. I'm responding to what feels like flashes

of…not memory, maybe intuition. And I'm responding to you the way I am, because sometimes I have
the distinct feeling that you're holding back something I should know.''

Drew looked at Laura. When he spoke, his voice
was gruff. ''I'm not holding back anything you need
to know. I want your memory back as much as you
do. More, even. But I'm trying to be careful not to
inundate you with a lot of useless information that
will only confuse you.''

She took a tiny step closer and tilted her face up.
''Maybe I should be the judge of what's useless information.''

''I don't know if you can.'' He let out a heavy
breath. ''I don't know if *I* can, either.''

She was quiet for a moment, then she asked, ''Does
that mean you're giving up on me?''

He turned and looked into her large, luminous eyes.
Laughing blue eyes, even at a time like this. ''I'm
close,'' he said, but he couldn't help smiling. How
many years had it been since Laura had been as open
as she had been these past two days? He'd almost
forgotten this side of her.

''Could you wait until we've got this life thing of
mine straightened out?'' she asked.

''We'll get you straightened out no matter what.
I'd never leave you.''

''Oh, yeah? Can you promise that?'' She tried to
laugh.

''I already did promise that. I married you,'' he
said softly, looking at the woman he'd promised the
rest of his life to eight years ago. What had happened
to that? Just a year and a half ago, that promise had
been hanging by a thread. Had they really changed

so much from the people they were when they first fell in love?

Yes. They had. And the tensions had mounted relentlessly. Habits of mistrust, suspicion and apathy had been formed. Eventually they'd ended up on the road to doom and they couldn't turn around.

Then Laura had "died." And Drew had fifteen months to think about how differently he could have done things.

A lump formed in his throat. "I promised for better or worse, as I recall."

She raised her hand to his cheek, and stroked the scruff he hadn't had time to shave that morning. "This can't be the *better* part for you."

"Your coming back is the best thing that ever happened," he vowed. "And from now on, things are only going to get better."

She didn't look convinced. "I hope that's true."

"I'm going to make sure it's true."

She smiled and brushed his hair back at the temple with her thumb. "I do apologize about the earring. It took me off guard and, like I said, I've been so insecure about taking my life back. But I trust you." Her thumb brushed across the corner of his mouth.

He lifted his hand to hers and his groin tightened. He closed his eyes for a count of three and when he opened them again, she seemed even closer than before. "You trust me?" he repeated. That was something he hadn't heard from Laura's lips for long months before she'd gone.

"Yes." Her voice was quietly insistent. "I don't know why but I do."

He put his hands on her shoulders and pulled her to him. The time apart had obviously changed things for Laura, too. She'd gotten to spend fifteen months playing the role of a women whose self-esteem had *not* been pounded down. He hoped this new confidence would stay with her even when her memory returned. "But not enough to move back yet," he said.

She stiffened and he realized, even before she spoke, that he'd gone too far. "No. I'm sorry, I can't promise that will *ever* happen."

His throat constricted, but he didn't let on how much her words hurt. "I'm not asking for that promise." He ran his fingers through her soft hair. Laura sighed in a way he recognized. She'd always relaxed under a light touch.

"I hope not." She swallowed, drawing his eyes to her throat. He wanted to put his lips to the spot.

Instead, he lifted her hands to his mouth and kissed each wrist lightly before holding her hands against his pounding heart. "But if you decide you *want* to..."

She gave a hesitant nod. "Okay. I'll keep that in mind."

Her words were casual, but her eyes told a different story. Her eyes said she was holding back more than ever. Something must have happened to put that hesitation in her eyes. Maybe some memory or fragment had come to her. There was something she wasn't admitting.

He knew that look; he'd seen it before. For long weeks before she'd disappeared.

After her disappearance he'd been tortured by questions. He knew—he *knew*—in those last months *something* was really bothering her, but she refused to talk about it. She'd grown colder and more distant

by the day and there was nothing he could do to stop
it.

It had driven him to the breaking point, and when
he'd told her his decision she had only nodded, word-
lessly. They'd never talked about it. If she'd had feelings about it, she'd hidden them and hidden them
well.

Of course, he could hardly blame her for that now.
Now that he was keeping such a big piece of the
puzzle from her.

Laura went through the rest of the house in a daze.
The earring thing had been an embarrassment, to say
the least. If she had taken even a moment to look at
it she would have seen it was cheap metal, bent
askew, and the gold was chipping off. No self-
respecting woman would have worn it to impress a
man she was interested in. And Drew wouldn't have
gotten involved with a woman who didn't have self-
respect.

As she followed him from room to room, she found
herself wanting more and more to touch him. She
wanted to feel him against her, to feel his arms around
her, his fingers on her skin. It was difficult to understand. She'd never had that sort of impulse in her life.
At least not in her memory. At the shelter, everyone
had teased her for being so immune to attractive men.
While others were fawning over videos of the hottest
Hollywood stars, she would actually be watching for
the plot. And she was about the only one.

Well, she was making up for it now, with a full-
blown schoolgirl crush. On her own husband.

Now, so close to Drew, breathing in the scent of
him and feeling the electricity that hummed around

him, Laura was undergoing feelings she didn't recognize. Desire. But not just desire—this was *appetite*.

Fortunately or unfortunately, he didn't share the feeling. He was obviously trying to keep some distance from her. Every time they started to get a little bit close physically, he backed off. For the moment that was probably good, but if it kept up this way, Laura thought she might go insane.

If she wasn't already.

They stopped at pictures on the wall and little knickknacks on tables and shelves. Drew explained where they'd come from and occasionally the story behind a purchase. Like the glass coasters with brightly colored mosaics of dolphins and windmills they'd gotten in Greece. According to Drew, a shopkeeper had taken a fancy to Laura and piled gifts on her, including the coasters, a cotton blanket, several obscene-looking Greek fertility icons and a brass bottle opener with a cross on top.

Nothing was familiar to her but everything felt unusually comfortable. Sam's room had drawn a blank, but also a longing. She wanted to know what it felt like to cuddle up on that lacy soft bed on winter evenings, reading *Goodnight Moon,* while snow fell and wind howled outside the dormer windows.

She must have done that. But there was no picture of it in her mind.

It was hard to believe she could have forgotten all of this. Did she know, before the accident, how *lucky* she was? Over the past couple of years she had learned to not even dream of a life like this, because the dream was so unlikely to come true.

Yet here it all was. And Drew was telling her that it was hers.

After a while, Drew went downstairs to pour some ice teas while Laura meandered back through the bedrooms, taking her time with them. She knew he didn't care about the tea, he was just giving her time alone to absorb everything. He was very sensitive, she thought with some pride. A really thoughtful man.

The idea that he'd been having an affair was probably just some paranoia cut and pasted from an old suspense movie she'd seen. Maybe the Grace Kelly one in which Grace's husband tried to have her killed while she was talking on an old-fashioned black telephone, like the one in her reading room. That was probably all there was to it.

Laura spent about twenty minutes milling through the rooms and was on her way downstairs when she heard the doorbell ring. Drew's footsteps thumped across the hardwood floor and she heard the door squeak open. She stopped in her tracks and clutched the banister, replaying in her mind the grind and squeak sound of the door opening.

That was familiar. Of all things, that was definitely familiar. She even anticipated a final metallic click just before she heard it. For a moment she stood there, heart pounding and fingers gripped painfully around the banister. She remembered something! Was it all coming back to her? She waited quietly for a moment but nothing happened.

She let go of the banister. She was getting carried away. It was just a door opening, for heaven's sake. They all sounded pretty much alike.

She continued down the stairway and heard Drew saying, "Oh, Jeez, Adele. This *really* isn't a good time—"

Adele? Laura's spine went straight and her limbs

filled with ice. Who was Adele? Why did that name give her chills?

A woman's voice cut him off. "Nonsense, Andrew. You didn't return my call yesterday or this morning. Either something's wrong, or you're just plain rude. Which is it?"

"Neither." His voice grew hushed but Laura could still hear him plainly. "I'm working on something that I—I really have to get back to. It's really important. In fact, I haven't had time to do anything else. Or even think about anything else," he added.

"Huh."

Whoever the woman was she wasn't any happier about his excuse than Laura was. Working on *something*, indeed. If Drew was so crazy about his wife, if he was as devoted as he swore he was, why was he lying to this woman about her?

"I mean it, Adele. I'm going to have to call you later tonight."

"I'm here now. Why wait for tonight? Come on, out with it."

"Not now."

"Fine. If you don't want to talk, then you can just listen. I'm sure this won't be a surprise to you—in fact it's crossed my mind that this is the reason you've been avoiding me. That child needs to go to boarding school. I've said it before, and I'll say it again. The school system here is nothing like what you'd find in that school in Virginia."

"I'm not sending Sam away. Period. Thanks for your input, though. I'll see you later."

"I'm not leaving until you agree to this. *Samantha* needs to go."

That was it. Whatever this woman's relationship to

Drew, Laura was back and no one was going to make decisions about her child for her. She took a steadying breath and walked down the stairs. If this was her home she should act like it.

"Adele, please," Drew was saying. "You've got to go. I can't explain right now, but I will soon. Honestly."

"What behavior!" the woman snorted. "You'd think you were building nuclear bombs in the basement." Her shoes clip-clopped across the floor, away from the front door.

She obviously wasn't leaving.

Well, good. Laura wanted to meet this *Adele*. Moreover, she wanted Adele to meet *her*.

"Adele—"

"Drew?" Laura called, in a cheerfully innocent voice. "Where are those drinks you were getting?" As soon as she stepped into the room she saw him. His face drained of all color.

"Oh...my...God." That was the woman's voice off to the side, but it sounded more like a rush of air.

Drew closed his eyes.

Suddenly feeling like *it* in a game of freeze tag, Laura turned to look at the person to whom Drew had been too embarrassed to admit his wife was back. The woman who had the unmitigated gall to try and send her child to another state. What she saw surprised her.

The woman was much older than she'd supposed, perhaps in her mid- to late sixties. She was tall, and quite stocky. Her salt-and-pepper hair was swept back in a short cut, and her eyebrows, which at the moment were close to her hairline, were penciled in. Her eyes were pale, watery blue and surrounded by white, like those of a scared animal. Her mouth was drawn into a wide O.

"Oh my God," Adele repeated. "My God."

Laura echoed the words in her head. She didn't know what she had walked in on but it was apparently not what she had thought it was.

Drew rushed to the other woman. "Adele, I was going to tell you about this, but I only found out yesterday myself and I thought it would be best if—"

"Laura?" the woman asked, looking straight into Laura's eyes. "Laur..." She began to tremble violently. "It's a spirit! Andrew, can you see her? She's right there next to the piano."

"I know—"

"She looks *alive*," Adele rasped. "Talk to us, spirit, don't disappear! Where are you?"

This was insane. Laura had experienced her share of strangeness over the past year, but this took the cake. The woman plodded toward her, arms outstretched like a sleepwalker. Laura took a step backward, but she couldn't find her voice.

"Come on, Adele, stay calm." Drew slipped his shoulder under the hefty woman's arm and half carried her to the couch while Laura stood watching helplessly. She thought she should help but she couldn't move.

"Let me go!" Adele shook herself off of Drew and turned back to Laura. Then she walked slowly toward her with her beefy arms outstretched and shaking. "I must see her, one last time."

Laura threw a frantic glance toward Drew. *You couldn't just stay put?* his expression seemed to be saying. He went back to Adele and tried to slow her determined march toward Laura. "Adele, listen to me! That's Laura, but she's not a ghost. She's alive, Adele. It was all a mistake. A huge mix-up.''

"Alive? She's not alive. I went to her funeral.''

She couldn't help it. Laura laughed, drawing startled looks from both Drew and Adele. "I'm sorry,'' she said, trying to sober herself. "But you people put *way* too much faith in circumstantial evidence.''

The woman's expression changed and her face grew paler. But Drew's expression was actually one of amusement. A smile played at the corner of his mouth while he looked at her with a gleam of what looked like admiration in his eyes. After a moment, he turned back to Adele.

"What Laura is trying to say was that it was a mistake,'' he said. "Her car was apparently stolen that day, she was mugged, hit over the head, and she's had amnesia ever since. Someone else died in the car.''

Adele didn't appear to be listening to him; she just barreled forward toward Laura.

Drew stopped the woman and turned her by the shoulders to face him. "She doesn't remember us.'' He was practically shouting. "She doesn't remember Samantha, she doesn't remember me, she doesn't remember you. We hope that will change but right now I think you're scaring—''

"What do you mean she doesn't remember me?'' Adele snapped.

"Sit down,'' Drew said, indicating the wingback chair Adele stood next to. "Sit down!''

She sat.

Drew took Laura by the arm and urged her over to the couch with him. They sat side by side, and he laid a warm hand on top of hers. The reassurance from that small gesture spoke volumes. Without stopping to think about it, she twined her fingers in his.

He noticed, of course, and turned to her with the briefest smile. It was the sort of a movielike moment that made women swoon in the old days. Laura herself felt her pulse drum madly. It wasn't just the way he looked, it was the way he looked *at her.* As if he really *saw* her.

She hadn't felt that from anyone before.

Drew turned his attention back to Adele. "Believe me, I know this is a shock for you. As I told you, I was going to tell you just as soon as Laura was secure enough."

"This is *real?*"

"Yes, it's real."

"And you've known since yesterday, without telling me? Don't I have a right—"

"Laura's health is more important than anyone's *rights,*" Drew said harshly. "Imagine how traumatic this must be for *her.*"

Heat pulsated from his body, warming her bare arm. Until now, the sleeveless tank dress had seemed appropriate for the weather, but Adele had brought a chill into the room that went right to Laura's bones.

"Laura, darling, talk to me." The watery blue gaze was focused on her now. "Tell me you remember me." She barely waited a moment before snapping, "Tell me!"

"I'm sorry, I can't. I don't remember..." Laura gave Drew a questioning glance.

He gave her a sympathetic look and murmured, "Laura, this—" he made a weak gesture toward the woman "—is your mother."

Chapter Six

Laura weakened. The last traces of her good humor disappeared. "My mother," she repeated. Her heart turned into a boulder and dropped to the pit of her stomach. "Mother." The word felt new to her. She had assumed she didn't have parents. Why?

"I would have thought at least *you* would have let me know," Adele said to Laura.

Laura looked at her blankly. Whereas she'd felt a stab of familiarity or at least interest when she first saw Drew, Adele sparked no feeling in her at all.

It should have been a tremendous joy to meet her own mother but this...well, this wasn't what she would have expected. Mothers were gentle, sweet, loving, understanding people like Barbara Billingsley on that old show "Leave it to Beaver," or Jane Wyatt on "Father Knows Best." There were hundreds of shows on TV that had mothers on them. None of them were loud and demanding like this one.

Of course, she realized that TV wasn't exactly the

most reliable measuring stick, but it had to be based on *some* truth, didn't it?

Laura stopped. Maybe her judgment of Adele wasn't fair. After all, she'd only just met the woman. Still, it was a bit unnerving that her mother was more concerned about them keeping secrets from her than she was about seeing alive the daughter she'd believed dead for so long.

"...that this is exactly the sort of trauma I was trying to prevent for her," Drew was saying.

"Mmm-hmm." Adele drew herself up in her chair and turned to Laura. "Tell me, Laura dear, how did Samantha react to seeing you again?"

"I haven't met her yet." She hesitated, waiting for the reprimand she was certain was coming. Adele had probably never kept an opinion to herself, and she was clearly not a person who would understand, much less agree with, Laura's terror of traumatizing her child.

"Not met her?" Adele turned an annoyed gaze to Drew. "What have you been doing? Hiding her in the broom closet? How on earth could Samantha not have seen her if she's been here since yesterday?"

He looked exasperated. "Laura is staying at Starbuck House for now," her hero defended. "It will be less traumatic for Sam if we take it slowly."

"Now you sound just like that father of yours," Adele scoffed. She lowered her chin and raised her tone. "I suppose once you've lived with a psychiatrist you can't help but sound like one, but I am a student of the real world and, believe you me, the sooner Samantha has her mother, the better."

"That could throw them both into shock."

Ignoring Drew, she looked pointedly at Laura. "A

good mother always knows what's best for her child. That doesn't go away with any amnesia."

Laura found her voice. "Drew and I talked it over and decided that I see the house first, then meet Sam in it so as to avoid both of us going through the shock of it at the same time."

Her mother snorted. "Since when does Andrew Bennett listen to someone else's counsel? It seems to me you couldn't even get him to go—"

"That's enough!" Drew said, standing up. "Adele, you're going to leave now."

"You can't kick me out at a time like this!"

"I can if you're going to upset Laura."

"Ahh, I see." She raised a superior eyebrow. "You haven't told her everything, have you? How very convenient for you, Andrew."

Laura's ears perked up. "What's convenient?" She straightened and turned to Drew. "What does she mean you haven't told me everything?"

He kept his narrowed eyes on Adele. "She means... I'm not going to do this with you right now, Adele." He shook his head. "Not at Laura's expense."

"Surely you can't be suggesting that *I* would try to hurt Laura," she sputtered indignantly. "But I think she ought to know—"

"She knows." He turned to Laura. "There are a few things we haven't talked about yet, but Adele is alluding to our personal problems." His gaze slid to Adele and back. "The ones we talked about earlier."

"I see." Laura doubted it ended there, but she also knew that she'd rather eat bees than hear this woman's version of events right now. "We've talked about that already," she said to Adele.

Adele was taken aback. "And it doesn't bother you anymore?"

Laura's mouth went dry but she pressed her lips together and said, "We're trying to move *forward*."

Something in Laura withered. Drew *was* keeping something from her, exactly as she'd suspected. And it was clear that he wasn't going to tell her what it was. Laura didn't know who she and Drew were before the accident, and obviously Drew didn't want her to know.

After another fifteen minutes of poking and prodding and trying to reassure herself that Laura was, for one thing, alive, and for another thing, honestly amnesiac, Adele finally left. However, she had first made the ominous pronouncement that she would see Laura *alone* at the next opportunity.

Laura had agreed just so the woman would leave. The novelty of having a mother had worn off quickly in the face of Adele Singer's overbearing ego. She couldn't get off the topic of how difficult it was for *her* to cope with Laura's presumed death and sudden reappearance *without so much as a telephone call.*

Drew had offered kindly to drive her home, in consideration of the shock she had undergone, but she insisted on driving alone.

"At least," she had said, "I can count on myself, unlike some other people."

When at last he closed the door behind her, he turned to Laura and said, "I'm sorry."

She shook her head. "No, I'm sorry for laughing earlier. I just couldn't help it, but she did look angry, didn't she?" She gave a small chuckle.

Drew smiled. "I think she came within an inch of telling you that you were grounded."

Laura laughed and flopped onto the couch. "I'm stunned. Are you sure that's my mother?" Her eyes were lit with uncharacteristic amusement.

"You feeling okay?" Drew asked.

"Fine. Why?"

"Usually you're in a black mood for hours after a visit with your mother."

She looked surprised. "Seriously? I let her bother me?"

"Immensely."

"Hmm. Maybe amnesia isn't an entirely bad thing, then. Gives one a little perspective. Adele's overbearing but she can't have any more power over me than what I relinquish to her."

Drew walked to the couch. "This is amazing. You're so relaxed, so forthright. You rarely used to say what you thought, especially if it was negative. You were raised to be so polite."

"Ugh." She leaned back against the pillows on the couch. "I think I'm starting to understand why I married so young."

"Hey." He sat down next to her, but resisted the incredible urge to touch her. "You married young because you met the only man on earth for you and you knew there would never be another."

She slanted her eyes at him. "Yeah, well, if he's so wonderful, where is he *now?*" She laughed.

The sound of her laughter was like music. She was so relentlessly lighthearted that it carried him right along with her. "First sign of trouble and he was outta here." He jerked his thumb toward the door. "Now you're stuck with me."

She gave him a coy look. "How will I bear it?"

Drew looked at her, unable to keep from smiling

like a fool. He couldn't remember ever feeling so happy. The visit from Adele had been uncomfortable but it seemed to have established a new camaraderie between the two of them. He knocked her playfully in the arm. "You're going to have to muddle through somehow."

There was a moment of comfortable silence, then Laura said, "Drew, why *did* we get married so young?"

He recalled the start of their courtship, the day when eighteen-year-old Laura rode her bike past his house six times before he finally came out and she pretended to be "just passing by." He'd loved her from that moment on, though he hadn't known it for a while. "You were twenty, I was twenty-five. That's not so young."

She raised her eyebrows and gave a small shrug. "I think it is. I mean, what do you know at twenty?" She laughed then, but it was hollow. "Come to think of it, what do *I* know at twenty-nine?"

He was touched by her resignation. "What do we ever know? The older you get, the more hindsight you have, that's all. Everything in life is still a gamble."

She didn't look convinced. "I wonder why I felt confident gambling with something so big when I was so young." Her eyes met his and a softness stilled her features. "Or maybe I don't wonder," she said softly.

"You—" he pointed a finger close to her lips "—were in love."

She caught his hand and held it. "Can you prove that?"

A shivering silence passed as they looked into each other's eyes. Drew's groin tightened, and all the muscles in his body seemed to stiffen in response. He wanted her. He wanted her so badly, he was an inch away from tearing her clothes off and having her on the coffee table, on the floor, on the stairs, in the hall and, finally, on the bed in the sleepy afternoon sunlight. But he had to resist those impulses. The books had been very clear on how stressful it was to overstimulate.

"Mmm?" Laura looked at him expectantly. "Nothing to back up your claim?"

I'd love to prove it to you. He cleared his throat. "I have letters from you." Think baseball, he commanded himself. The Red Sox. Anything but the way she was looking at him now. "Old letters."

She not only looked surprised, but pleased. "You saved my letters?"

He shrugged. "I'm a sap." He flashed a slightly self-conscious smile. "But if you tell anyone, I'll deny it."

"Ah, your secret is safe with me." A silence passed. She took a breath, then another. "Drew?"

He traced his finger across her knuckle. "Hmm?"

Something made him look up, and when he did, her face was etched with concern. "What was Adele getting at earlier? About us?"

He'd been dreading this.

He kissed her hand, then leaned back against the couch and regarded her. "You really want to talk about this?"

"I don't *want* to, but I think we should."

He studied the orange horse on the mantel. "You asked before if we had marital problems."

"And you didn't exactly answer."

He hesitated for a long moment. He didn't want to

get into this right now. "Because it didn't seem necessary to bring up the bad things in our past when we have this golden opportunity to get to know each other all over again without all that baggage."

"That's just the thing. You have all the baggage. I don't even have a lunch box. I can't help but feel you have an advantage over me."

"This isn't a competition."

"I know it isn't but still you have control of our relationship because of it."

"Is it necessary for you to focus on remembering the negative?" He moved toward her slowly. "Why not remember the good things? There were so many good things."

"There has to be a balance. I'm sure you're getting tired of me saying this, but I don't remember *anything*."

"Maybe you think you don't." He cupped his hand on her cheek. "But do you remember this?" He slid his hand through her hair, to cup the back of her head, and pulled her gently to him.

The heck with discretion, he needed this.

They needed this.

When his lips touched hers, Laura felt a current buzz from her chest straight down to her toes, setting off some flutters in her stomach along the way. Her response was automatic and she closed her eyes.

He moved closer still and clasped his other hand around her shoulder. She ran her hands along his chest, over his broad shoulders, and folded her arms around his neck.

A voice in her mind wondered what on earth she was doing. She hardly knew this man, he was a stranger and she was fairly throwing herself at him. But that voice belonged to Mary Shepherd. Now she was listening to another voice, deeper inside. The voice of Laura, or of Laura's heart, telling her that she needed this emotional and physical nourishment right now more than she needed food and water.

So she followed the strange compulsion of her instincts, determined to see where it took her. He felt so powerful in her embrace, and she felt so safe in his.

At first their kisses were small, tiny explorations, but both Laura and Drew grew hungry quickly. The small kisses slowed and deepened. On instinct, Laura parted her lips, welcoming Drew's tongue and meeting it with her own.

The sensation was exquisite. She'd never quite understood the whole "melding of souls" concept, but with a single kiss she felt her very life force sinking into Drew, like an anvil in quicksand.

Somewhere in the back of her mind, she thought that if she didn't stop it, she might lose herself. Then she remembered that she was already lost, and at this point could only find herself. She pulled closer to him and their heartbeats synchronized.

Drew's hands trailed down her back and pressed suggestively against her lower back. The thrill was as strong as if he was touching her bare skin. She thought she should feel more cautious but she didn't. After all, she had nothing to lose and everything to gain by this. She arched toward him like a cat, as his fingers traced up her back, then around to her breasts.

For a moment suspended in time, she held her breath. Then, when he slipped his hands inside her bra, she sighed heavily, expelling all the tension in one breath. The inner voice of Mary Shepherd ceased its objections and her intuition was reassured that this was *right*.

Inside, she trembled with anticipation. Her body yearned for Drew. She wanted his hands on her, all over her, lower and lower until...

She sucked in a breath at the thought.

Drew pulled back. "I'm sorry, I didn't mean to push you too far."

"What?" Laura focused on him, more than a little disoriented. Why had he stopped? "Did I do something wrong?"

"You?" His eyes widened. "You didn't do anything wrong at all. As a matter of fact, from where I sat, everything was just right."

"Then why did you stop? Why do you pull away from me every time we get close?"

"I'm a stranger to you."

She laughed. "You're my husband."

"But you don't know that."

She trailed a finger down his chest. "I believe you."

"The psychology books," he said in a voice that strained to be objective. "They were very specific about not overstimulating the amnesiac."

She laughed. She couldn't help it. "At this point I'm so *under*stimulated that it would take months before you could cross that line to *over*stimulated, as you like to say."

"But the stress—"

"Drew."

His concentration was broken. "Yeah?"

"I don't think it's like me to be forward," she said, raising a brow in query. "But this feels more right and sensible than anything I've done over the past year. All my logic got me nowhere until I followed my intuition and ended up on Nantucket, so I'm thinking my intuition is pretty reliable. Besides that, I'm an adult. You worry about your decisions and let me worry about mine, okay?'' She laid a hand gently, and very deliberately, on his upper thigh. Just centimeters away from the increasing bulge in his jeans.

He squared his shoulders. She saw him swallow. ''Do you know why a baseball diamond is shaped like a diamond?''

''No,'' she said, inching her body closer to his.

''It's—'' She moved her fingers slightly closer and he closed his eyes. ''It's very interesting....'' He forced his eyes open and looked at her evenly. ''If you're going to worry about your decisions, this might be a good time for that because one more minute and I can't be responsible for what I do.''

Her gaze shifted over his features, stopping at the lips she'd thought so much about over the past day. They were slightly swollen from the fervor of their kisses. Laura put her finger to them, then leaned in and pressed her lips against them.

Drew moaned and pulled her back into his arms, running his tongue along the outline of her lips before thrusting it into the dark warmth of her mouth.

She leaned back, taking him with her, his body melding over the length of hers. She felt his hardness against her. Her body flamed like a fire in the wind.

Contrasting the frenzy of desire she felt, she slowly lifted her hand to his head. Her motions were deliberately lingering, stringing out the mélange of sensations that hummed from her heart to her groin. Drew's hand brushed across her hip, her behind and around to her inner thighs. Tingles spread across her skin like ripples on a pond.

Laura sank deeper into the dark pit of longing and ran her fingers slowly through his thick hair, aware of every sensation from her fingertips to her toes. He moved his hands to the front of her dress and started unbuttoning it carefully, pausing every once in a while as if to ask her consent. She arched her back, offering herself to him, and felt the hot breath of his sigh against her cheek.

His kisses grew harder, hungrier. His tongue thrust deeply into her mouth and circled her own, teasing, tantalizing, no longer asking a question but making a bold statement. *Yes,* her fog-filled mind repeated over and over. *This is right.*

I've missed this.

It was a fact she was certain of. The sensation was exquisite, not to be compared with any other desire she could recall.

His mouth left hers and trailed kisses across her jawline. She arched her neck and felt his light kisses dot down her throat. Then his fingertips flicked lightly across her shoulders and pulled the material off. He pulled back for a moment to look at her, then ran one fingertip across her breasts and down to the snap of her bra. It flipped off before she could think, and his hands were upon her, squeezing the pliant flesh until she was incapable of thought.

"You're so beautiful." His fingers danced lightly across her belly and slipped inside the waistband of her underwear. "It's been so long."

Laura heard her own intake of breath and held it while his movements edged softly downward and slipped into her. He held still for a moment and she wondered vaguely if it was his pulse she felt pounding through her core, or her own.

Then he started to cajole her desire into desperation. His fingers moved in ways she couldn't keep track of, making her feel things she had never even imagined. Pleasures of varying intensity chased across her chest and into the pit of her stomach. More than once she found she wasn't even breathing. He played her like a fine instrument.

Black and white and red swirled behind her closed eyelids, then an explosion of color. An image nudged its way into her mind. Not quite a memory but more a reflection of a memory, like a shadow on the water. Dark amber sunlight pouring through a window. These kisses, this weight on top of her. Dark hair tinged deep red where the light touched it. His skin was deeply tanned. Eyes of midnight brown, fringed with dark lashes, heavy with passion. She drew a shuddering breath.

"Satch." She didn't realize she'd said the word aloud until he pushed back and looked at her with shock.

"What did you say?"

"I—I don't know. It just came out." She searched her mind for the word or its meaning but all she came up with was an echo of what she'd heard herself say. "Satch? I don't know what that means."

Drew sat up and looked shocked. "I do."

She blinked, still groggy with her body's yearning. "Okay, what?"

He looked at her like she was a ghost. "You used to call me that. Ages ago."

"I called you Satch?"

He colored. "It was sort of a joke at first."

"What does it mean?" She raised her eyebrows, expecting an explanation that would make sense of it.

After a long pause, he shrugged. "Nothing much. I've always loved Louis Armstrong so..." He let his words trail off.

When he didn't continue she said, "Can you elaborate?" Louis Armstrong. Who was that? An astronaut? She searched her mind and a picture came to her. A singer. Louis Armstrong was an old-time singer of some sort. "Was he a singer?"

"That's right. A singer and a trumpet player. How did you remember?"

She shrugged. "I didn't. I just...knew."

By now Drew wasn't looking at her, he was looking *into* her. "I can't believe you said it." He shook back to attention. "Satch. Satchmo. That was his nickname."

An idea too bizarre to believe came to mind. "And...are you saying I used to pretend you were Louis Armstrong when we made love?" she asked incredulously.

"Sometimes." He looked at her evenly. "Other times we'd pretend I was Sonny Bono and you were Cher."

Laura regarded him in stunned silence, then burst out laughing.

"You've always been so gullible," Drew said with a laugh.

"Oh, good, then it's not true."

He shook his head, still smiling. "No, it's not true. You know how nicknames are. They start as a joke and eventually the *reason* behind them is irrelevant. Really, Laura, I would think you'd have more faith in your sense of self."

Her eyes gleamed with humor. "It was *you* I was worried about. Don't you worry about my sense of self."

"Honey, you keep that attitude. That's about the *only* thing you can be sure of right now. That and me." His low voice was warm with sincerity.

She paused, trying to make sense of it. Why had she said that name? Quietly she looked for the place in her mind that had clicked back enough for her to recall it. But she couldn't—it was gone.

Drew's lips curved into a rakish smile. "Mrs. Bennett, it would seem that perhaps you *can* be overstimulated."

"Touché. But the memory, or whatever it was, is gone." It occurred to her that perhaps if they made love again it would come back to her. "I didn't know what it was when I said it and now I don't even know *why* I did. It's just…gone."

"No," Drew said. "No, I've seen more glimpses of the real you than I did in the last year of our marriage. You're laughing again, you're not taking life so seriously. It's wonderful. Your old self isn't gone, it's just hidden. And I believe now more than ever that we can uncover it."

She raked her eyes across his body and down to where his hardness still throbbed behind his jeans. With the greatest care, she touched the spot and looked into his eyes. "It's just going to take work, work, work."

His eyelids dropped to half-mast. "I'm up for it."

Then the clock over the mantel chimed twelve. For a moment it didn't register, then Laura gasped and said, "Oh, my gosh. It's twelve."

He glanced at the mantel, looking a little disoriented himself. "What do you turn into at noon?" Drew asked, touching his finger to the hollow of her throat, then running it down her breastbone.

"Didn't you say Samantha comes home at noon?"

He straightened immediately and looked at his watch. "Noon. That's right."

Laura scrambled to her feet. "I've got to get out of here. She certainly can't see me like this."

"I'm not too crazy about her seeing me like this, either," Drew said. "Let's see, I have to think about something else. A distraction. Baseball, baseball, the Yankees won the World Series in…" He looked at Laura. "God, you're beautiful. You're more beautiful now than ever."

She smiled, thinking he looked pretty darn good himself. "Thanks, but you're nuts. My hair's a mess, my clothes are all rumpled." Her eyes flitted again to the clock: 12:05. "I've got to go." She hurried to the front hall and snatched her purse off the hall table.

"I'll drive you."

She hooked her purse over her shoulder. "No, no. You stay here for Sam." He looked skeptical and she added, "I could use a bit of walking to clear my head anyway. Please."

He followed her to the door and reached into his pocket. "Here's cab fare."

"No." She touched his hand. "Thanks. I have it."

"You sure?"

She searched his eyes. "I'm sure. I'll walk into town and catch a cab there."

He was obviously resigned. "I'll call you tonight."

"Okay," she said, a little breathlessly.

He shook his head. "Why do I feel like we're in

high school all over again? Look, why don't you just stay here and we'll tell Sam tonight?''

Her heart ached. ''I'd love to, but I know I'm just not ready. Not yet. Tomorrow.'' She slipped out the door before he could stop her.

When she got into the warm sunshine, she took a deep breath and tried to steady herself outside of Drew's presence. It wasn't easy. She could smell him on her own skin. But it was a delicious scent that carried a delicious memory with it, and that would see her through the night.

She heard voices behind her and turned to see a woman and a little girl with shiny copper hair. They were farther up on the sidewalk, walking straight toward her before they turned into Drew's house.

Laura's heart missed a beat. Another piece of knowledge came to her without benefit of memory. Any lingering thoughts of Drew melted away from her mind. In the center of it all—the center of Laura's life and heart, she realized—was the love for her child.

Her eyes burned with the strain of trying to see what she was too far away to see. The child inside— the essence of Samantha. Laura was certain that if she could only recognize that, she would recognize everything else.

''Daddy!''

That single word, sung in the high childish voice, pierced a hole in Laura's heart.

The child bounded through the gate calling, ''Daddy, I'm home! Guess what I did today?'' There was an eruption of giggles as she disappeared behind the bang of the front door.

Laura closed her eyes. She thought she could hear

her voice inside, but the wind picked up, obscuring it. Maybe once this wind had carried the word *Mommy* in that same voice, up that same front walk.

Guess what I did today? Laura couldn't even hazard a bad guess. So removed was she from the life of her daughter that she didn't have any idea what she did during the day or what might have excited her enough to run home and tell Daddy.

Did that mean she was a bad mother? Logic told her no, but her gut argued that a good mother would *never* forget her own child, no matter what.

A good mother always knows what's best for her child. That doesn't go away with any amnesia. Adele's sharp words cut right through Laura's consciousness. She hadn't realized at the time how pointed they had been. But were they true? Laura searched for an emotional reaction to Adele but found none.

No, she thought in a pleasantly detached way. They weren't true and they didn't make her feel bad because she was going to have a different relationship with her daughter than her mother did. Laura was going to have a close, loving relationship with Samantha, no matter what else happened.

It might not be the kind of relationship Adele would have preferred... Laura almost laughed. Why take to heart the words of a woman who was trying to manipulate? Somewhere inside she knew that once the sentiment from her mother would have wounded her, but the person she was at this moment saw Adele as a cartoon villain—not truly evil but not truly kind, either. And definitely not to be taken seriously.

The fact was that Laura was only hours away from the most important moment of her life—or at least of her new life. She was hours away from a reunion with her daughter. After that, life would no longer be the same. There would always be at least one place that she *belonged*—with her child.

Apart from that, there were no hard and fast rules or definitions of a "good mother," Laura decided. Except to love and care for her child and to vow always to do the best she could. Amnesia didn't make her a bad parent. She loved Samantha; she knew that even if she didn't *remember* it the way she would have liked.

If she didn't regain her previous relationship with Sam, she would forge a strong new one. She had absolute confidence in herself and Samantha on that point at least.

Her relationship with Drew was another story. She would have liked to have the same confidence in that, but there were so many unanswered questions. She hoped her relationship with Samantha would come naturally. But the answers about Drew, she knew, would not.

She was going to have to work for that.

With that personal mission in her pocket she turned to head back to town when she heard the creak of the front door opening, then the bang of the screen door. Laura turned to look.

Samantha stepped out onto the porch and skipped down the walkway, her shoes clicking lightly. Her movements were like dancing, and they exuded the happiness of childhood. The breeze carried the tuneless song she sang. No words, just light hums. She stopped to pick up a newspaper and skipped back to the house with it.

Laura watched with bated breath. An instinct to run

to the child and take her into her arms assailed her. It came from nowhere but felt as strong and reasonable as the impulse to step out of the path of an oncoming car. Laura sank her teeth into her lower lip. If she approached Sam now she would be treated like a stranger. Sam might even be frightened of her.

So Laura stayed still, offering a silent prayer for the strength to wait until tomorrow.

Samantha stopped suddenly. She couldn't have heard Laura's plea, yet for some reason she turned and looked directly at her.

For a shivering moment their eyes met across the distance. Time stopped. Even the wind disappeared for that one expectant moment.

Then...everything was normal again on the outside. The cars hummed in the distance, petals drifted off a cherry blossom tree onto the path before her and birds kept singing. It almost seemed as if some great chance had been lost and she spent a moment wondering what she should do next.

She looked back at Samantha, who had taken a few more steps toward the house. Then, as suddenly as she had before, she stopped and turned back.

Laura's breath left her in a rush. She didn't know what she expected, but it surprised her when Samantha waved.

Laura raised a shaking hand in response, and smiled, hoping that, at this distance, it wouldn't look nearly as tremulous as it felt.

Sam gave a fleeting smile and went back into the house, swinging the newspaper in her hand as if she hadn't a care in the world.

Chapter Seven

On the morning she was to meet her daughter for the "first" time, Laura woke up at five. It had been a restless night anyway, but by five her mind was racing with thoughts and she couldn't get back to sleep. So she lay in her hotel bed, with her own home not far away, thinking about the fact that she was a wife and a mother.

She had promised her *life* to two people and had no memory of it.

No cognitive memory, that is. As the hours ticked by, she became more and more aware that she did have feelings for them. Very strong feelings. With Drew, it had begun with what she could only label "instinct." The moment she'd laid eyes on him, something had called to her, but it was in a language she didn't understand. As she'd gotten to know him some over the past couple of days, the feelings had grown. Fast. She didn't know if they were based on memory or if she had a brand-new crush on the man, but the chemistry was undeniable.

Unfortunately, there were a lot of questions that couldn't be ignored, either. Questions about their past together and how that tied in with her ''disappearance'' fifteen months ago.

With Samantha, though, Laura's feelings were different. Intuition told her she loved the child without reservation. There was a huge swell of love in her, with nothing muddy or convoluted about it at all. It was the association that was vague. Without remembering the child, the feeling was a painful longing inside of Laura that didn't have any place to go.

Today it would be returned to its rightful place with Samantha. Today, surely, Laura would at least remember her own child.

And if she didn't...she couldn't stand the thought. She'd cross that proverbial bridge if and when she came to it. And if that happened, Drew would be there with her, he would help. He knew them both, and he'd know what to do if there was an unexpected problem.

When seven o'clock finally rolled around, Laura got out of bed to get dressed. She planned to get to Drew's—to get *home;* she couldn't get used to the idea—at eight. She took a shower, then changed her clothes three times. None of her mousy bargain-basement outfits seemed right for the occasion but they were all she had. Finally she settled on a simple blue cotton dress and leather sandals.

She was getting ready to pick up the phone to call a cab when it rang. It was Adele, pressing her for a commitment on when they could get together. Laura evaded her as best she could by talking about her plans to meet Samantha.

The conversation went comparatively smoothly until Adele hit her with "I'm glad you're taking the divorce business so well. I must say, I'm surprised."

Divorce? Laura's chest tightened. "Y-you're surprised?" she managed faintly. For a reason she couldn't quite name—again she called it "intuition"—she was determined not to let on how much or how little she knew.

"Well, I shouldn't be surprised," Adele said airily. "You had a while to get used to the idea."

Laura swallowed. Was Adele referring to Laura and Drew? Or her own marriage and some possible trauma Laura had suffered relating to that?

Drew certainly hadn't said anything about divorce. Surely he would have if it were true. No, Adele must have been talking about something else. Maybe herself and Laura's father. "*You're* divorced?"

"Why, yes." The surprise in her voice verified Laura's suspicion. As in *Of course. What have we just been talking about?*

"I'm sorry," Laura said, ignoring a creeping discomfort that warned there was more to this. "Is he— Does he live on Nantucket, too? My father, I mean?"

"No, dear, your father passed away some time ago now." The voice was impatient.

Laura searched for sorrow or some sort of void but came up with nothing. "I didn't remember."

A sigh hissed across the wire. "Yes, yes, you've said that. Tell me. When will we be able to talk, just the two of us? I'd rather not do it over the telephone."

Do it. That sounded ominous. "Soon. I can't say

exactly when, what with meeting Sam and reacquainting myself with 'home,' but soon.''

''And, of course, all the details you and Andrew will have to work out, poor dear. What a lot to do all at once.''

There it was again, that insinuation that something wasn't right with herself and Drew. The creepy feeling returned, and she thought again of the divorce Adele had mentioned. Could Laura possibly have wanted to divorce Drew? It didn't seem right somehow. Besides, that would have been one of the more important details he would have given her up front.

Or would it? If she wanted to divorce him, that might well be something he wouldn't want to remind her of.

Laura didn't want to ask Adele about it. She wanted the truth and she wasn't at all sure that was what she'd get from her. ''We'll talk about that another time, all right? I've really got to run.'' She didn't wait to hear her mother's sputtering protests. ''Bye for now.''

She set the receiver back with a decisive click. She'd heard enough negativity from Adele. Whatever the truth, it wasn't going to come from a woman who had such obvious disdain for her son-in-law.

And it wasn't going to come from Drew, either. He seemed so glad to have her back, she didn't want to remind him of any intention she had to leave unless it turned out to be necessary. She'd have to find out why. And it was something she was going to have to discover for herself.

By the time the cab pulled up in front of ''her'' house, Laura's heart was pounding ridiculously.

Once, this had been a daily event for her, seeing her husband and her daughter. Now nothing seemed more remote or frightening. More than once she had an impulse to tell the driver to turn back, but when she thought of Drew's gentle reassurance and steadying presence by her side, her nervousness subsided.

Drew was already outside, and he hurried over to her when she got out. He handed the driver a bill and waved him on before Laura could even reach for her purse.

"Show-off," she said.

He smiled but it was fleeting. "I wanted to impress you. Look, I spoke with the psychologist and she suggested that you have a few easy, social meetings with Samantha before we tell her who you are. That way her feelings will have a little time to develop normally without the pressure of love versus feelings of abandonment."

Abandonment. The word itself was painful. She hated the idea that she had abandoned her own child, whether she'd intended to or not, though she couldn't even imagine intending to. "All right," she agreed. "We'll do it that way."

Drew let out a pent-up breath. "Yeah, well, we'll see if it works."

"Why shouldn't it?"

"No reason. It's just that things never seem to happen the way the experts think they will. Doesn't matter, though. We'll handle it."

She narrowed her eyes. "You're nervous, aren't you?"

"No, of course not. What's to be nervous about?" he said, but it came out rushed.

"Yes you are." She stopped and looked him squarely in the eye. "Why?"

"I'm not. What makes you say that?"

"Your smile was distracted, you're talking really fast and your eyes are sort of...twitching."

This time he did laugh. "*Twitching?* I don't twitch."

She raised an eyebrow. "Yes, you do."

He sighed. "Okay, I'm a little nervous. I don't know how Sam's going to react to this. I don't know how *you're* going to react to this." He ran his forearm across his brow and looked toward the rising sun. "Hell, I don't even know how *I'm* going to react to this."

Laura nodded and said, with composure that surprised even her, "Then we should probably go on in and get started, rather than standing here speculating and worrying." She took a long breath. "If I don't go in now I may lose my nerve."

He took her hand. "Don't do that. We'll get through this."

She studied his face, his eyes. He looked so sincere. She wondered again if she could have ever actually wanted to divorce him. "How well do you and Adele get along?" she asked suddenly. "Under normal circumstances, I mean."

He looked surprised. "Why?"

"Just curious."

One side of his mouth lifted in a wry smile. "I gather Adele has let her maid's fingers do the walking and she called you."

Laura raised her eyebrows. "You're evading the question."

He puffed his cheeks full of air, then blew it out.

"All right. It'll be obvious before long if it isn't already. We're not best friends, Adele and I. But we've stayed in contact because of Sam."

"Was she against our marriage?"

He screwed up his mouth and pretended to think about it. "Well, if you call canceling the order for your dress behind your back, begging the minister not to condone the union, burning the honeymoon plane tickets and sobbing throughout the ceremony being 'against' the marriage, then, yeah, I'd say she was against it."

It might have been funny if it weren't so obviously the truth. Laura frowned. "Why was she against it?"

He let out a long sigh. "You come from a wealthy family. A *very* wealthy family—Newport, the Hamptons, all of that. She's used to controlling everyone and everything around her. You were bulldozed by her for years before you finally stood up for yourself, and when you did it really got to her."

"So by interfering in our wedding plans she was trying to manipulate me just for the sake of manipulating me?" Her stomach began to ache. Maybe this explained why the thought of motherhood had been a difficult one for her since the accident.

"I don't know," Drew answered. "She may have believed I was after the family fortune."

Laura raised an eyebrow. "Were you?"

He looked around the room. "Are you asking because you're suspicious of the palatial surroundings?" He laughed.

"No." She smiled. "I can't really see you as a gold digger," she said, but her stomach continued to twist. "But still…" She concentrated, trying to bring her intuition into language that she could make sense of. "It seems important. To us, you and me."

"It should. It took years for you to be able to entertain the idea of marriage. Your parents' marriage terrified you. Hell, it terrified me, too."

"Why?"

"It terrified you because your father's philandering was accepted as normal in their circles. Your theory was that your mother couldn't control him so she controlled you instead." He looked like he was going to continue, then stopped and looked deeply into her eyes.

"So my theory about getting married to escape wasn't necessarily that absurd."

He considered for a while before finally shaking his head. "I can't believe that. It took me a year to persuade you to take the plunge. I think ending up like your mother was more of a threat than living with her." He hesitated, then shrugged. "But all I know is what you've told me and what I can guess from knowing you."

I'm the only one with all the answers. I may never know. "Tell me this. Did Adele try to sabotage our marriage once it was legal? You know, manipulating behind the scenes or anything like that?"

He paused and cocked his head. "Where are you going with this?"

"She told me that..." It was on the tip of her tongue to say, "she told me we were headed for divorce," but she stopped herself. "That we had some problems, that's all. You heard her. I just wondered if she might have an ulterior motive for it."

He considered. "Much as I'd like to say yes, I can't believe that she'd try to manipulate this particular situation." He scratched his chin. "Then again, I wouldn't be surprised. But, just to be safe, if you have any questions, ask me."

He started to lead her toward the house but she laid a hand on his forearm to stop him and asked, as casually as she could, "Did I have a close friend?"

Again he hesitated, as though he didn't want to tell her. "Yes, you did."

"Care to elaborate?"

He didn't make a face but he might as well have for the negativity that was oozing from him. "Her name's Dawn Whitford. She lives in Boston now. I was thinking I'd have to call her and tell her about you, but I've been putting it off. As soon as she hears, she'll probably be up on the next plane."

Dawn Whitford. The name meant nothing to her. "What does she look like?"

He shrugged. "Light blond hair. Blue eyes, I think. Maybe brown."

Immediately Laura remembered her first day in the house, and the incident with the business cards. The woman in the picture—what was her name? Gena Finley. She'd had pale, pale hair and eyes, and it had spooked Laura tremendously. Did she remind her of Dawn? Was that why?

Laura swallowed her anxiety. "Were we very close, Dawn and I?"

"Yeah, pretty close."

"But you didn't like her." This she knew. She didn't know how, but she knew. He felt strongly about it.

He gave a humorless laugh. "You may not recall anything, but your perception sure hasn't changed. You're just as sharp as ever."

"Thank you." She tilted her head. He was pretty sharp, too. "And you're quite competent at evasion."

He looked at her evenly. "Dawn and I used to be friends, through you. But after your accident we drifted apart. Our common interest was gone." He splayed his hands. "That answer your question?"

"I guess so." She sighed. "But it raises a heck of a lot of others."

"I'll tell you what—"

Before he was finished, the front door crashed open, giving them both a start, and Samantha came running out. Laura thought her heart would stop. This was her child, her flesh and blood. Not so long ago she'd nursed her, changed her diapers, stayed up nights to feed and soothe her.

Now she didn't know her.

"Daddy!" Pink sneakers thumped on the cement. Her face was alight with excitement and her bright eyes were focused solely on her father. "I have something to show you!"

With a glance at Laura, Drew turned to Samantha. "Something to show me? What is it?"

She was aglow. "There's a dead mouse in the basement."

Drew bent down to her and brushed a strand of hair back from her eyes. "What's it doing?" he asked with a teasing smile.

Sam looked at him with a lowered brow for a minute, then burst out laughing. "He's just lying there, Daddy. Can I pick it up?"

He straightened. "Not a good idea. I'll take care of it later. Right now I want you to meet someone." He stood up and reached for Laura's hand, reassuring her with his warm gaze.

For the first time Samantha seemed to notice Laura standing there. She turned to her, auburn hair gleaming in the sunshine, and light blue eyes as clear as a baby's. She was so lovely, such a bright light.

Laura hoped the stark contrast of her trepidation wasn't written all over her face, but she was pretty sure it was.

"Hello," Sam said guilelessly. With a very straight face, she gave a clumsy attempt at a curtsy. "I'm Samantha Bennett. What's your name?"

Laura swallowed hard. Her breath rattled through her with no depth. She looked uncertainly at Drew, then knelt before Sam. "I'm…Laura," she said tentatively.

Samantha tilted her small chin upward and screwed up her face. Laura trembled under the scrutiny.

After long moments Samantha finally said, "Oh, I remember *you.*"

Laura's stomach twisted. She met Drew's equally surprised gaze, and he gave a barely perceptible shrug.

She turned back to Samantha. "You do?" Her voice was barely more than a whisper.

Sam's nod was enthusiastic. "Yes, you're the lady that was there yesterday."

Laura's whole body hummed, but disappointment suffused her anticipation. "Yesterday?"

Sam pointed to the spot on the sidewalk where Laura had stood watching Sam and the baby-sitter come home. "You were right there."

Laura's heart sank. Sam remembered seeing her as she'd left yesterday, not from years of motherhood. What had she expected? That a child of four, who hadn't seen her in fifteen months, would remember her? It was preposterous. "That's right. I saw you come home."

Samantha continued to look at her curiously.

"So..." Laura was as nervous as a girl on her first date. But that was her role yesterday. Today she was a mother. Who knew what she would be tomorrow? "Did you have a good time at school yesterday?" she asked awkwardly.

"Yes. Then I got to make dinner for Daddy."

Laura smiled, refusing to allow the thought that she had interfered with Sam's day by being with Drew the night before. "Ahh. Do you always make dinner for him?"

Sam shook her head. "Only sometimes. We have peanut butter on crackers. But he has to help."

Laura took a breath and knelt in front of the child, exactly at eye level. "You're quite a young lady, aren't you? Going to school every day then coming home and taking care of your daddy. He's very lucky to have you."

"We don't have a mommy." Sam said that with a sidelong glance at Drew. "But I *used* to. A long, long time ago."

Laura swallowed. In the corner of her eye, she saw Drew make a move toward them slowly. "It's been hard not having a mommy, huh?" she said, watching the child as carefully as the child seemed to be watching her.

"I miss her." The answer was carefully measured and drawn out, and Sam frowned, inadvertently crinkling her nose. Then she reached out and touched her fingertips to Laura's cheek. "You look like a mommy."

A rush of emotion swept through Laura's body,

lifting her heart into her throat and burning water into her eyes. She lifted her hand to Sam's and held it there.

But before she could formulate a response, Sam said, "Do you want to see my flower garden?"

"Yes, I'd love to." Laura stood up and reached automatically for Sam's hand. "Where is it?"

"In the backyard."

Laura looked at Drew, who appeared somewhat bewildered but pleased. "I'll, ah, I'll go get some lemonade and take it out," he said awkwardly. "You two go on." He gave Laura a reassuring nod. "I'll be out in a minute."

"Come on." Sam tugged on Laura's hand. "This way."

With one last nervous glance at Drew, Laura followed the child around the side of the house to a pansy garden lining the back wall. There were other flowers, too—sweet William, marigolds, four-o'clocks, sweet alyssum—Laura wasn't sure how she knew the names, but she recognized them immediately. They carpeted the garden in uneven clumps, making the child's garden even more charming for its lack of precision.

"This is lovely," Laura said. "Did you do all this yourself?"

"My mother and me made it when I was a baby," Sam informed her, with a return of that curious look. "Don't you remember that?"

Laura didn't have one moment to react to that, much less answer, because Sam continued on, enthusiastically, "I don't remember because I was a baby. Daddy helped with the spanzies last week, aren't they pretty?" She reached down, picked one and put it to her nose. "It smells good. Here." She held it up to Laura's face.

Laura took the flower from the child. The light brush of her fingers against Sam's hand made her heart trip. Had they been in this very spot before, doing the same thing they were doing now? It wouldn't have been the same. Sam would have been much younger then, just past babyhood.

Laura concentrated on remembering something, anything, but nothing came to her.

"It smells delicious," she said, reaching over and tucking it behind Sam's ear. "Now you look like a proper island girl."

Sam laughed and picked another flower. "You can wear one too." She held it out and Laura took it. "Now we're *both* island girls."

"We are," Laura agreed, reflecting on the heaviness of the truth. They were both Nantucket natives. This earth, this patch of land, was *hers*. Her home. She looked at the yard, the clean-cut green of the yard, the faded flagstone patio, the black wrought-iron patio furniture. It was the kind that waffled your skin in the summer when you sat on it in shorts.

Now how did she remember that?

"Daddy says they like to be picked and they grow back even faster when you do," Sam said, gathering a handful of them.

"Then we should pick a whole bunch of them and put them all over the house, shouldn't we?" Laura laughed, picking a handful herself. "Or decorate the patio. How about this?" With Sam at her side, she took her small handful of flowers to the patio table and started dropping them one by one through the holes so that just the faces showed on the tabletop. "This will make the prettiest table in town."

Sam laughed delightedly and followed Laura's example.

Soon they were getting along wonderfully, like a mother and daughter who had never been separated. By the time Drew came out forty-five minutes later, they had filled the entire tabletop, as well as most of the chair seats, with the small colorful flowers.

They didn't notice him come out—without the lemonade he'd said he would get. There hadn't been any and he wasn't quite sure how to make it from scratch.

Laura and Sam were placing their flowers with the utmost care, and talking with great seriousness about the problem of butterflies having to go through life looking like flying flowers and always confusing people.

Even though he knew she didn't realize it, Drew saw that Laura was a natural with Sam. Just like she'd always been. And Sam was clearly adoring—he'd never seen her take to anyone quite as quickly and completely as she did with Laura. It was probably safe to go ahead and tell her the truth, despite the fact that the school psychologist had recommended waiting.

Watching Sam with Laura now made Drew realize just how much Sam had missed Laura over the past year. Not that he hadn't known how much the child missed her mother; he just hadn't known how much she'd *needed* her. He'd worked so hard to pay extra attention to Sam that it never occurred to him that there were certain things he wasn't capable of providing for her.

Her mother's touch, for example. Her mother's soft

understanding. Her mother's sweet, intuitive compassion. It had always been so. Laura was soft where he was hard; she was emotional where he was logical; she was patient where he was driven. Those balances were important. They accounted for Sam's tendencies toward math like her father and art like her mother. They accounted for the Lauraesque stubborn streak in Sam as well as the diplomatic peacemaker that was so like Drew. They accounted for a million things, large and small.

And they meant that Drew *couldn't* be both mother and father to her no matter how hard he tried and no matter how much he loved her. That didn't make him a failure; it made him human like everyone else.

He turned his attention back to Laura and Sam. They were grouping the pansies by color now. Sam had a delight in her eyes that Drew hadn't really seen before. Did she somehow instinctively realize that Laura was the mother she'd lost, or was she so starved for a mother figure that she took instantly to the first woman, besides Mindy, who came along?

There was a shriek of childish laughter, and pansy petals flew through the air. "It's snowing!" Sam laughed again. "It's Christmas!"

No, there was magic at work here. Somewhere inside, Sam knew she was with her mother. Maybe it was time to tell her the truth.

"Hey, you guys," Drew said, calling attention to himself. "What's going on out here?"

"Daddy!" Sam dashed over to him. "Me and Laura are having Christmas. See the snow?"

He smiled and reached down to scoop her into his arms. "Christmas! But it's almost Mother's Day!"

Laura did a double take and he realized that might

not have been the thing to say under the circumstances. He shifted Sam in his arms and turned to Laura, mouthing the words, "Let's tell her now."

Laura's gaze lingered on him for a moment, then she gave a nod.

"Sam," Drew said. "We have to have a talk. Let's sit down, okay?" He glanced at the table and chairs covered with flowers, and plopped her down onto the steps. He sat next to her and extended an arm, beckoning Laura.

Laura stood still for a moment, then went and sat on the step in front of Samantha. She didn't look to Drew for reassurance this time, but took Sam's hand in hers and said, "This may be a surprise to you, but I hope it's a happy one."

"What's the surprise?" Sam wanted to know.

Now Laura looked to Drew. Her eyes were unusually bright, and her lips were drawn in a tight line to keep from crying.

"Sam." Drew took a breath and put a hand across Sam's shoulder. "This is going to sound like a story, but it's absolutely the truth, okay?"

"Okay."

"You remember how there was an accident with Mommy's car last year, and how Mommy didn't come back."

Sam nodded. "You told me she was in heaven."

Drew swallowed. "I thought she was. We all thought she was. But somehow Mommy got out of the car *before* it crashed."

Sam kept her eyes glued to Drew's. "So she didn't die?"

"That's right." He smiled. "She didn't die."

Before Drew could tie the ends together and present Laura in a logical way, Sam turned to her and said, "*You're* my mommy."

A quick breath jerked through Laura. She closed her eyes but tears came spilling out anyway. After a long moment of trying to gain control, she looked back at Sam and said in a strangled voice, "Yes." She opened her mouth as if to continue, but only managed another shuddering breath before pressing the back of her hand to her mouth and closing her eyes against tears again.

"Why didn't you come home?" Sam asked, heedless of Laura's inability to answer.

"Sam," Drew said gently, drawing her attention back to him. "It's not that simple."

"Why *not?*"

"Mommy didn't die in the crash but she was hurt. Badly. It's taken her all this time to get well enough to come back to Nantucket."

"Why didn't you call me?" Sam asked Laura.

"Samantha," Drew said. "This is going to be really hard for you to understand but you're going to have to try. I promise you it's the truth. Mommy was injured on her head and it caused...it affected..." He let out a tense breath. "She was hit so hard that it knocked her memory out. She didn't know who she was. She forgot everything."

"Even *me?*"

Drew nodded. "Even herself. She didn't even remember her name."

To Drew's shock, Samantha giggled. "That's not true! No one forgets their name."

"Sam!"

"It's okay." Laura's voice broke the tension. She was finally smiling although with a sniff. "It *does* sound crazy," she said to Sam. "But you know what sounded even crazier? Daddy coming up to me in the street and telling me I had a family and a house right here."

Sam frowned. "Weren't you here to find us?"

"I guess I was," Laura said slowly. "But I just didn't know it. All I knew was that I wanted to come to Nantucket, but I had no idea I'd find you and Daddy."

This made Sam laugh again. "Did you think you were an orphan?"

"Yes, I did. So finding you is like a fairy tale."

Sam frowned. "Which one?"

Laura laughed and mussed Sam's hair. "I don't know. A new one. Our own fairy tale."

Sam smiled, obviously pleased at being the star of her very own fairy tale. "I want to be Cinderella."

"But I like you an awful lot as Samantha," Laura said.

"Okay." Sam's smile fell. "Oh-oh. I just remembered."

Laura's features jerked into a frown. "What?"

"Your toothbrush isn't here anymore." She looked at Laura very seriously. "You're going to have to get another one. Do you have underwear?"

Drew laughed, causing two pairs of concerned eyes to turn in his direction. "I don't think you have to worry about that stuff, Sam. Mommy already thought of that sort of thing."

Sam looked relieved. "It's important," she said authoritatively. Then she turned back to Laura. "Can I go to your room with you and help you unpack your suitcase?"

Laura went white.

Drew felt like he'd been punched in the stomach.

"Sam." He cleared his throat. How could they have been so foolish as to not prepare for this obvious assumption on Sam's part? "Mommy's not—"

"I don't—"

Drew and Laura looked at each other, alarm mirrored in their eyes.

"Mommy still doesn't remember living here," Drew said, knowing that no matter what he said, it was going to sound like an insufficient reason to Samantha. His mind raced but no magic words came to mind. "So it's like a brand-new place for her. It's sort of scary to move into a new place without getting used to it first."

Clearly Sam didn't understand a word of what he'd just said. "Mommy lives here."

"Not right at this moment," Drew said uncomfortably, floundering in the void of what should have been a logical response. "Like I said, it's new to her and—"

"It's an *old* house," Sam said to Laura, looking to her for a more reasonable answer than her father was producing. "Don't you want to come back?"

"I—I don't know," Laura stammered. "I'm staying with Mrs. Flanders at Starbuck House now. Do you know her?"

Sam shook her head.

"Oh, she's very nice. You and Daddy and I can go visit later and meet her, if you want."

"Where am *I* going to sleep?" Sam asked.

Laura looked blank.

"You're going to sleep in your room, where you always sleep," Drew said. His voice weakened when he added, "Right here with me."

Sam put her elbows on her knees and set her chin heavily in her hands. Then she turned to Drew and said something he'd never even imagined she'd say, raising an issue he hadn't thought about in fifteen months.

"I want to go live with Mommy."

Chapter Eight

Drew felt his blood drain to his feet.

A year and a half ago, when he'd started divorce proceedings, he might have expected this. He *had* expected this. Laura would have custody and he would have visitation and some weekends, holidays and whatever else the standard agreement consisted of. At that time—which now seemed like a lifetime ago—it had made the most sense. Laura, after all, was the primary parent. Drew had merely been the family supporter, the financial anchor to Laura's more important emotional anchor.

Put more bluntly, Drew had been an insensitive jerk. He'd passed off the parenting duties to Laura completely while he worked night and day. His family had been important to him, of course, but until Laura's disappearance, he hadn't realized how *precious* it was. Until Laura's disappearance, he'd had no idea what a comfort and pleasure his own child could be.

It hadn't taken long to learn, and now he'd had fifteen months for those feelings to strengthen. He could not give it all up now.

He could not control Laura's actions, he realized. He couldn't *make* her stay with him. But he couldn't let her leave and take Samantha, too. It was unthinkable that the elation and hope of Laura's return would turn into the horror of losing *both* of them.

It would kill him.

Or, worse, it would force him back onto the path he used to take. He couldn't be that same man again, he thought, because now he knew, now he *appreciated* the gift of a child.

He looked back at Laura and Sam, now hugging tightly.

"I'm not going away," Laura was saying. "You have your mommy back for good now."

"But you don't want to live with us," Sam protested, her voice breaking.

Concern was etched in Laura's features but without confidence. "Now, Sam, I didn't say that I was never going to live with you again...." She looked to Drew with questioning eyes.

"Sam, honey." He knelt down beside the child. "Like I said, Mommy doesn't remember her life with us yet. Maybe someday she will, but now it feels to her like she's just met us."

"But she's my *mommy*," Sam cried, looking at Laura with tears in her eyes. "I don't want her to go away."

Drew saw Laura wince and blink back the watery shine in her own eyes.

How could they not have talked about *this* possibility? It was his fault; he should have anticipated it.

Naturally, Sam wasn't going to understand why her mother, returned from the dead, wasn't moving back home. He barely understood it himself. He searched for a response, but before he could think of one word to say to her, Laura spoke.

"Then I won't go away," she said. "I'll stay right here with you."

Samantha smiled through her tears, as only a child can. "You will? Really?"

Drew's thoughts echoed Sam's words.

"Yes, I will." Laura looked at Drew, a trace of a question in her expression. "I'll just have to pack my things and bring them over from Mrs. Flanders's place."

"Today?" Sam asked excitedly.

Laura's eyes lingered on Drew's for a moment before she turned to her daughter and said, "Yes. This afternoon." She looked at her watch. "It's almost lunchtime now, so I'll do it after that. And you should probably go get cleaned up before we eat." The instruction seemed to come naturally enough to her, but immediately she turned to Drew with raised eyebrows, as though to ask if what she'd done was okay.

"That's right," he said to Sam before the hesitation could cause Laura any doubt. "Run along now."

Sam bounded into the house, her movements alive with joy. It had been so easy for her—she'd accepted Laura back as if she'd only been gone for a day. Drew's anxious anticipation of trauma was unnecessary, as it turned out.

He looked at Laura. She looked considerably more uneasy than he would have liked. "I should have seen that question coming," he said. *Did your decision, any of it, have anything to do with me?* he longed to ask.

"I thought that, too, for a moment, but really, what other answer could we have given her that would have made her smile again?"

Is that the only reason? "You're probably right. She wouldn't have accepted your not moving back home."

"Like you did?" Laura said lightly, watching him.

"I didn't exactly *accept* it," he said evenly. "But I don't have license to scream and object the way a child can. That doesn't tend to work as well for adults."

"Hmm."

What in the world did that mean? "Did you *want* more of an objection from me?" It was a loaded question and he knew it but he couldn't continue to second-guess Laura's every move and word.

"That would be childish," she answered noncommittally.

"Maybe. But did you?" It was on the tip of his tongue to ask, "Would that make you feel more loved?" But he stopped himself. That would have been the old Laura. This was the new one.

She smiled at him. "Would I normally need that sort of cajoling?"

Once again she'd read him like a book. Was there any point in lying? "It had gotten to that point," he admitted. "But normally, no, you had much more self-confidence than that."

She appeared to consider this. "You know, I really have no patience for people like that, people who need everyone to go out of their way to accommodate them. It's a wonder you put up with me."

"I loved you." *Liar*, he thought. He was deliberately misleading her. He'd loved her all right, but he'd stopped putting up with her insecurity, hadn't he?

She raised an eyebrow. "That isn't always the answer to things like that, though."

"No. It's not."

After a moment of quiet, Laura said, "About moving back into the house…"

"I know it's because of Sam," Drew assured her, certain he knew what her concern was. "You don't have to come back to our bed." He hesitated, questioning the wisdom of telling her his preference. She knew, of course, already.

She gave a nod, then said slowly, "It's not *only* because of Sam."

Drew's stomach twisted. "Laura, I'm not very good at guessing what you mean these days. Are you saying—"

"I'm saying I want to be with you, too."

Her newly rediscovered bluntness was a great thing. She didn't add that she was wary, but he saw it in her eyes.

Hell, he felt that way himself. But he was willing to take the chance. And now, it seemed, she was, too. "Are you sure?" he asked. "Really really sure?"

"Yes," she said softly. "I'm sure."

To Laura, her return home later that evening held a strange ring of familiarity that her other visits had not. Of course, by this point she *did* recognize the house, but there was more to it than that. Their conversation about her parents had somehow freed her from some of her confusion. Until that point she'd felt pain when she thought of marriage and parenting.

She'd worried that the feeling was a warning about her own life, yet when they'd talked about her parents, the fear somehow evaporated.

Now her response to returning home was more positive, excited. Passionate. As if she didn't just recognize it, but loved it, too. It felt like *home* in a way nothing ever had before.

And Drew, who was helping her with her luggage as well as the mental hurdle of leaving Starbuck House while a baby-sitter took care of Sam, was showing many more facets than she'd originally believed were there. Slowly but surely he was becoming less of a comfort and more of an intrigue to her.

At first she would have been lost without his quiet strength to guide her. Now, as her confidence grew and she wasn't as uncertain as she had been initially, she began feeling things in her heart that she'd never felt before. She was aware of the possibility that the feelings were merely a new infatuation with a very attractive man, but her instincts told her it was more than that.

Her instincts told her it was love remembered.

But that didn't alter the fact that her need for Drew was becoming less emotional and more physical. Much more physical. All evening some electrical current had been buzzing between them. At times—like when he turned to catch her gaze and held it, or when her hand brushed against his leg in the car—it felt like an electrical shock. She imagined a voltmeter exploding from the intensity.

Now, as he shifted her suitcase from one hand to the other to get the keys from his pocket, her eyes lingered on his shoulders and the muscles rippling under his thin cotton shirt. Powerful shoulders, she thought. From real, old-fashioned physical work, not some shiny chrome gym equipment, if this landscaping was any indication.

Her hands tingled with the urge to smooth over the contours of his skin. *Tonight.* The word came to her as a fact, not an idea.

Tonight.

He must have felt Laura's gaze on him because when he opened the door to the house he turned back to her and said flippantly, "Are you waiting for me to carry you over the threshold?" He smiled, and in the dim glow of the porch light it reminded Laura of a devilish but romantic pirate in old Hollywood movies. The pirate would flash that rakish smile, then pull the lady into his arms, lower his mouth onto hers and...

"You underestimate my weight." She smiled but her heart was still gripped by the thought of his kiss.

He gave a quick shake of the head and stepped into the shadows of the porch with her. The wood creaked when he moved. She knew the sound. It went with summer and lemonade, and the bang of that screen door. It went with home.

It went, somehow, with being in love.

Drew ran his knuckle down her cheek and under her chin. "I carried you across once before. Remember?"

His closeness created a fever within her. She took a step back, toward the wall of the house, and swallowed. "No." He stepped closer, closing the small gap between them. "Tell me about it."

He leaned his fist against the wall behind her and looked down into her eyes. "It wasn't the crossing the threshold that was remarkable that night," he said.

The scent of him, clean soap mingling in the night air with light perspiration, was intoxicating.

Laura took a quick breath and clasped her hands behind her in an effort to avoid making any move toward him. Last time she had, he had resisted.

This time he could come to her.

"What was remarkable that night, then?" she asked in a voice that held more air than words.

"What wasn't?" He traced his finger across her lips. "For some reason, I've been thinking about this all night. I was thinking—I was *hoping*—that maybe you were dwelling on the same idea."

"I don't recall our first night here." She swallowed again, and blinked. *But my mind reels at the possibilities of our wedding night.*

He lowered his chin and light glinted for a moment in the seductive warmth of his eyes. He studied her for a moment, then cocked half a smile. "You really don't remember that night?"

Laura's knees began to buckle. They were playing a game, she realized, to see who could hold back the longest. "No, but if you hum a few bars..."

He moved in and gave her a long but chaste kiss on the cheek then rasped in her ear, "That night was the christening of the house." His meaning was as clear as sunshine through crystal.

When she looked at him she could feel the heat of her own gaze. "Of the house? Or the bed?"

He laughed. "The bed, yes."

She let out a breath and was about to try and change the subject to baseball when he continued.

"And the bedroom floor." He moved closer still and kissed her again, this time on the other cheek. "And the bathroom counter." His breath was hot against her ear. "And the upstairs hall. Not to mention the stairs."

"The stairs," Laura echoed, and leaned her head back with a wan smile. They'd played this game before—she knew it.

And she also knew she almost never won.

"The stairs," he said lowly. "As I recall, you liked that particularly. It was the perfect place for..." He lowered his head and trailed three kisses down the side of her neck. "If you want, I could show you what I mean."

"I can imagine," she said, and did, raising her temperature another several degrees. She doubted she'd ever go up or down those stairs again without imagining it. Heat coiled down her body like liquid and pooled in her center.

Then suddenly his mouth was upon hers, devouring her with kisses. *I won,* she thought vaguely, returning his passion with her own. *We both won.* If he hadn't given in to the temptation when he had, she would have. His kisses were like champagne, and she couldn't get enough. Her mind spun with ecstasy at the promise of emotional and physical fulfillment that lay ahead.

He wrapped his arms tightly around her, pulling her so close that his heartbeat felt like her own.

"Laura," he whispered.

She slid her hands slowly down his sides, stopping at the hip and letting her fingertips dance lightly toward the front. "Mmm?"

"We've got to get inside before we give the neighbors a show right here," he murmured into her ear.

Her fingers stopped at the desire that was tight in his pants. She smiled. "And just what do you think is going to happen between us, Mr. Bennett? I have it on good authority that I must be careful not to be overstimulated.'' She cupped his hardness through his jeans and gave a gentle squeeze.

Drew groaned. ''I don't think you're the one who's facing that particular danger right now.'' He pulled back and, before she knew what was happening, lifted her into his arms. ''But I'll try my damnedest, I promise you that.''

It was easy to believe. He crossed the threshold, and Laura said, ''But my suitcase—''

''Can wait until later,'' he said.

She laughed. ''And the baby-sitter?''

He muttered an expletive and at that moment, the baby-sitter walked in.

Drew set Laura down, but kept a heavy arm across her shoulder, holding her close to him and keeping her shrouded in contemplation of what was to come.

Somehow he managed to pay and dismiss the baby-sitter in what seemed like just moments. Sam was in her room asleep. They were alone. With one penetrating look and a flash of a smile, he said, ''I believe we were here,'' and swept Laura back into his arms, carrying her to the bedroom the way Rhett Butler carried Scarlet.

They didn't even bother with turning on the lights when they got to the bedroom. There was enough moonlight shining through the window to show the way. They stood beside it for several minutes, kissing deeply and fumbling with increasing frenzy to unbutton each other's clothes and slip them off.

Within moments they were on the bed, skin touching skin, their bodies bathed in the moon's silvery glow.

"Do you want this?" Drew asked lowly through the darkness. He traced his fingertips across her rib cage then moved them, tantalizingly slowly, down toward her navel.

"Yes," she breathed. "I'm sure."

He lowered his mouth to hers and kissed her fast and hungrily, then moved his lips across her throat and her chest, stopping at her breast. "You're sure?"

She arched toward him, with half an impulse to laugh and half an impulse to scream. "I'm *sure*." She tangled her fingers in his hair and pulled him toward her. "I'm really, really sure."

He flicked his tongue out, just barely touching her skin, then covered her nipple with his mouth, drawing such intense pleasure through her that she moaned.

She felt him smile against her, and move to her other breast, repeating his motion and her exquisite pleasure.

Slowly he returned his mouth to hers and kissed her deeply. Unable to wait any longer, Laura ran her hand across his solid stomach and beyond.

When she curled her fingers around him, Drew caught his breath. This time it was Laura who smiled with the satisfaction of knowing he wanted her as much as she wanted him. For a few moments they barely moved, then she kissed him again, locking her mouth against his, reveling in the delicious sensation of his tongue meeting hers.

Without breaking the kiss, Drew moved his hips toward hers. Instinctively she parted her legs. As he moved onto her, she opened herself farther, tilting her hips toward him.

She felt him nudge against her and moved her hips

to accommodate him. When at last he entered her they both breathed a heavy sigh.

Somehow she'd known that even though she couldn't remember their marriage with her mind, making love with Drew would help her remember with her heart. The feeling of completion that she'd anticipated came to her the moment they connected, and the confusion and questions no longer mattered.

Here was the answer.

Without hesitation or question, Laura's movements matched and complemented Drew's. The time that had been taken away from them ceased to matter as they melded body and soul, mending the uncertainty and doubt that had stood between them and their future.

The evening passed in a swirling sea of color, light and sensation for Laura. Wave after wave of pleasure coursed through her, nudging all traces of doubt with it. The past fell away like a dead tree branch, and left possibilities for growth that she'd never even dreamed of before.

When they were finally spent, Drew and Laura lay back on the pillows, deliciously drowsy, her head resting on his shoulder.

"Finally," he said. "Finally I know this isn't a dream." His fingertips skimmed across her back. "There were things I'd forgotten."

"Me, too," she said, smiling against his chest in the dark.

He laughed. "Yeah, well, there are also things you *haven't* forgotten, whether you know it or not."

"Good things?"

He yawned and pulled her closer. "Amazing things."

Pleased, she nuzzled in. "Worth waiting for, I hope."

"Darlin', you're worth waiting for even without those things." He kissed the top of her head. "I don't think you understand how much I love you."

Her heart skipped a beat. "As a matter of fact, you haven't said." She waited, taut with expectation.

He drew back and looked at her. "Is that right?"

"That's right."

"Hmm." He lay back down and pulled her close. A long moment passed.

"Drew?"

"Yeah?"

"Nothing. I…thought maybe you'd fallen asleep."

"Just about." He yawned again, then looked at her. "Was there something else?"

"No."

"Okay. 'Night."

A long moment passed and Laura cleared her throat.

Drew rolled over, his mouth clearly strained from holding back a smile. "I get the distinct feeling that you're trying to tell me something."

"I'm trying to tell you, damn it, that I'm falling in love with you."

His smile broke. "Well, I damn it love you, too."

Her heart tripped but she said with a straight face, "Oh, sure, *now* you say that."

His brow lowered fractionally. "Laura, I do."

She rolled onto her back and said, "Hmm."

"Greedy," he said, with a playful note in his voice. "You were always like that. Okay, do you want to hear about how I can't even fathom ever living without you again? How I'd walk through the fires of hell if it meant saving you?''

By now Laura's heart was fluttering like a moth at a porch light. She tilted her face up to look at him. ''I wouldn't mind hearing something like that.''

The corner of his mouth cocked into a smile. ''I cannot even fathom ever trying to live without you again.'' He kissed her other cheek. ''And if I had to, I would walk barefoot through the fires of hell, or worse, just to be with you.'' He kissed her forehead. ''Not that shoes would really do much good if you're walking through the fires of hell.''

Laura laughed and turned over onto her stomach, propping herself up on her elbows so she could look at him. ''Are you implying that I'll eventually be in hell and you're going to have to come from somewhere else to be with me?''

''Hey, if the wings fit—''

''Drew!'' She laughed.

He smiled back, then reached a hand up to cup her cheek. ''The truth is, Laura, that I loved you before and I love you still, but now... I'm more in love with you now than I've ever been in my life. And that's saying a lot.''

Tears burned her eyes. ''Do you mean that?''

''I mean every word of it.''

Nothing could have made her happier. She bit down on her lip to avoid bursting into ridiculous tears of joy. ''I feel the same way. I don't know if it's new, or more, or the first time, but I know I'm in love with you and I'll always be.''

She could have sworn she saw a sheen in his eyes before he pulled her back down to him and their words dissolved into the bliss of physical love.

* * *

When Laura opened her eyes again, the sun was just starting to peek over the horizon. The house was still silent. Drew was asleep at her side, as handsome as the devil but as peaceful as an angel. She loved him. He loved her. Things were finally *right*. She pressed a kiss to his cheek, then rolled out of bed to go down and have a quiet cup of coffee alone.

On her way down the hall, Laura stopped at the door to Sam's room and peeked in. The only window faced west, so the room was still cloaked in darkness, but the Jack and Jill night-light on her bedside table cast Sam in a warm glow. Laura saw the gentle rise and fall of her chest.

Laura sighed and walked quietly to the bedside. Her child, her daughter. The beautiful result of her love for Drew and his for her. In all her months in Connecticut, she'd never dreamed she could be this happy.

Samantha was as still as the stuffed animals on the bed with her, and she was more lovely than anything Laura had ever seen. Her long eyelashes were dark against her skin. Her closed lids were still and her brow was smooth and untroubled. She was the picture of serenity.

"Sweet girl," Laura said softly, bending over to touch the soft skin of Sam's cheek. It was warm and smooth, still rounded by babyhood. Her mouth was the same little bow it had been when she was born. She hadn't changed so much in fifteen months.

Laura froze. *She hadn't changed so much in fifteen months!* How had that thought come to her? And how did she suddenly know what Sam's mouth had looked like when she was born?

She looked back at the child and was gripped by another thought: Sam had all of her baby teeth now, but she hadn't the last time Laura had seen her. There was an image in her mind of Sam a little younger, pudgier, her hair still wispy like a baby's but the same color. But it was the smile that had changed. It was as if that small difference had drawn the line between familiar and unfamiliar.

Keeping her eyes steadily on Sam, Laura knelt by the bed and leaned in for a closer look.

The image in her mind changed, melting one face into another, and suddenly she was seeing a baby in her own arms, feeling her heartbeat accelerate at Sam's broad, toothless grin.

Then her own voice rang through the dark recesses of her mind. *"Drew! She just smiled! Come here quick. I swear she just smiled at me!"*

Barely able to breathe, Laura closed her eyes and concentrated. Her mind was suddenly racing, and her heartbeat with it. Time seemed to whiz by her consciousness, dropping only small tidbits to echo in her mind. A baby's laugh, the bang and bounce of the screen door, a child singing, a ringing phone, a car ignition turning over...

Pain. Shock. Laura tried to stop the memories but she couldn't. Voices rang like funeral bells, resonating deeply but incompletely.

"...so sorry...."

"...Mommmmmyyy!"

"I love you."

"...can't take it anymore!"

"...mine now. You don't belong in his life anymore. Why couldn't you just leave him alone and let us be happy...?"

"...Sam I am, Sam I am, Sam I am..."

It all stopped. As suddenly as they had come, the memories stopped their mad rush and disappeared back to wherever it was that they had come from.

Laura ran a shaking hand across her brow and was surprised by the clammy cold she felt there. She thought about the words she'd heard and tried to put voices to them but they had been so fleeting. More like reflections than memories, really.

But she had the feeling most of the words had been between her and Drew. Samantha was there, her childish voice crying out for her mother. And a woman's voice—was it the *real* Laura's? the woman she'd been before?—telling someone to leave "him" alone. Meaning Drew? *Was* he having an affair? And did her memories flicker past the point of confrontation with the other woman because it was just too hard to bear?

Then there was that phrase. It had haunted her in the hospital, the single thread that had linked her past and her present. *Sam I am.* It should have reminded her of Samantha but instead it was chilling. Why?

Tears filled Laura's eyes and tumbled down her cheeks. She didn't even try to stop them. Last night had been so perfect.... What lousy timing. Sniffing quietly, she kissed her fingertips and pressed the kiss to Sam's cheek, then got up and left the room.

Her heart heavy, she made her way back to the library that had once apparently been her private haven. Maybe there she could make some logical sense of this. She refused to let those fragments make her leap to the conclusion that Drew had absolutely been having an affair and therefore she had to leave him right now. It was a foolish person who crossed and burned bridges without knowing the facts first. Laura wasn't going to make that kind of mistake.

She flopped down onto the daybed and leaned her head back. Her heart was still pounding painfully in her chest and it occurred to her to wonder just what Drew's famous "overstimulation" could do to a person. The way those thoughts had rushed through her mind, out of control, had been frightening. What if it happened again? What if it lasted more than a couple of minutes next time? What if—

The phone rang, startling Laura out of her seat. She turned to face it, like a hunter facing his prey, with adrenaline coursing through her veins. It rang again. *No!* a voice in her mind screamed. *No! No! No!* She looked around her, half expecting to see someone else pick up the receiver and stop the incessant noise, but of course there was no one there.

It rang again. Drew obviously wasn't waking up. Laura's eyes flicked to the clock. It was just 6:00 a.m. so the call could be important. She had to answer.

She took a small, tentative step toward it, wondering at her growing agitation. The phone blasted again. *Do it.* She picked the receiver up between her thumb and index finger. It was cold and heavy but that didn't surprise Laura. What did surprise her was the fact that her hand was shaking tremendously as she placed the receiver to her ear.

"Hello?" The word had barely come out.

"Laura!" The woman's voice wasn't one she recognized, but it was tinged with familiarity. Could it be the voice of the woman she'd just been thinking of? The possible other woman?

"Who is this?" Laura asked, taking a breath to try and still the ridiculous fear that was growing in her.

"Laura, oh my God, I can't believe it's really you! I just got in, heard Drew's message, and there you are!"

"Drew's message?"

She didn't answer that. "Do you know how awful losing you was for all of us? Well, of course you don't. It was awful, Laura, really awful. Oh, I'm so glad you're okay, I can't believe this."

Laura hated to ask again, since the caller seemed to feel so close to her, but she had to. "Who—who is this?"

"Oh my God, it's true?" The woman clicked her tongue against her teeth, then said, "This is *Dawn*."

Laura's anxiety calmed slightly. *Dawn Whitford.* Her best friend. Drew didn't like her, but he'd left a message for her anyway, telling her Laura had returned. "Dawn," she repeated. "I—I'm sorry...."

There was an incredulous intake of breath on the other end of the line. "Drew said you have amnesia. Is it *true?*" She lowered her voice conspiratorially. "Or are you just, you know..."

It wasn't hard to guess what she was getting at. "Am I...faking?"

"*Are* you?"

"No! Is that the sort of person you think I am?"

"Not ordinarily, but you were so upset about the divorce—"

"Divorce?" The word was a blow to the gut, and for a long, strung-out moment, Laura trembled on the edge of a rush of tears.

"I mean, I knew you were desperate—I couldn't blame you—but I never dreamed you'd go that far."

"The divorce," Laura repeated. She was starting

to feel like a cheap parrot, repeating the word dully, almost in an effort to stave off a rush of emotion.

"You don't remember that, either?"

An ache crept slowly from her chest to her throat. She felt as if she might explode. "I don't know what you're talking about. Please...slow down." She swallowed hard. "There are just so many questions...."

Dawn chuckled over the wire. "Same old Laura, I see. Okay, shoot." She heard Dawn's chair creak, as if her friend were settling in for a juicy gossip session. "Ask me anything you want to know."

Here was the one person who didn't seem to have a stake in the outcome of Laura and Drew's relationship. It was a great opportunity. Laura took a steadying breath and switched the phone to her other ear. This numbness wasn't going to last much longer. She had to ask. "Okay. Was I...back when I left, when you thought I died—" she could scarcely get the words out "—was I divorcing Drew?" She held her breath, waiting for the answer.

"No way," Dawn said quickly and with the confidence of one who knows with certainty what she's talking about. "You didn't want that at all."

Laura let out her breath with relief. It was going to be okay, then. Whatever their problems had been, Laura hadn't wanted to divorce Drew. Things weren't as serious as she'd feared. Obviously they'd had some troubles, but at the bottom of it all, everything must have been okay with them.

"No," Dawn continued, oblivious to the impact she was capable of delivering. "You were devastated that *Drew* was divorcing *you*."

Chapter Nine

"**W**ake up, you jerk." Laura yanked the sheets back off of Drew, waking him with a start. "Wake *up*."

He tried to focus on her through sleep-heavy eyes. Was it a dream? "What's going on?"

"That's what I want to know, and I want to know *now*." She plunked down on the bed, facing him. The early-morning glow in the window behind her framed her in light, making her look like an oil-painted Madonna with an attitude.

"I've been sleeping," he said, wondering why he was steeling himself for battle in that old familiar way. "What the hell is going on?"

"I just got a call from Dawn," she said crisply, folding her arms in front of her.

Dawn! He sat up. This was no dream, it was a nightmare. He raked his hand across his hair. *Calm down until you know what she said.* He knew Dawn would cause some sort of trouble if he told her Laura was back. "How *is* Dawn?" he asked grimly.

Laura scoffed. "Pretty informative, as it turns out. Why didn't you tell me you were divorcing me?"

"Now, Laura—"

"Call me oversensitive but I think that's an important little detail you left out." She threw her hands up and stood. "What's the matter? Didn't you think I could handle it?"

"It's not—"

"Did you think you had to pretend to love me, to make love to me and pretend this was a real marriage so I could get well again?" Her face was scarlet. "What were you going to do then?"

"I wasn't *pretending* anything. If you would just listen—"

"Oh, so *now* you want to talk." He saw her hands tighten into small fists at her sides. "Now that you're in a corner, you're willing to put out a little bit."

"If you could take a breather, yes."

"Then do it." She walked toward the window, adding, "But don't waste your breath or my time with any more lies or evasions, all right?"

By now Drew was wide-awake and almost as angry as Laura appeared to be. "I didn't tell you about the divorce because it would have given you the wrong idea about my feelings for you. Hell, it *has* given you the wrong idea about my feelings for you."

"I can't even begin to imagine what your real feelings for me are," she interrupted, glancing back at him. "And I don't think you can, either."

He pointed a finger at her. "That's where you're wrong. There's where you've always been wrong. I told you how I feel and I meant every word of it."

"Which is, of course, why you were filing for a secret divorce." She turned her gaze outside. "It makes no sense."

"It wasn't secret."

"So you admit you filed for divorce?" She turned to look at him, and there was surprise on her face.

"Yes." He looked at her steadily. "I did."

Laura's face fell and she leaned back into the windowsill. Perhaps she hadn't believed it up to that moment, but there was no way he could deny it any longer. And there was little he could do to make her feel better about it. "I see," she said pointedly. "Because there was another woman."

He leapt from the bed, heedless of his nakedness. "That's a load of crap." He yanked open the dresser drawer and jerked a pair of underwear on.

"Is it? Or are you just a little bit afraid that I might have remembered something?"

He glared at her. "This is the part where you've caught me and now I'm supposed to confess to the crime and hang for it." He pulled a T-shirt out of another drawer and slipped it over his head. "Sorry." He splayed his arms. "I know it's a huge disappointment to you but there was no one else."

"I don't believe you."

He winced inwardly. The bliss of their reunion had evaporated and now they were back to being the bickering couple who had been on the verge of separation. "You always want to blame someone else for taking something away from you. The fact is that we—you and me *both*—screwed things up all by ourselves."

"Enough to divorce?"

"I thought so, yes."

"Then what's different now? Me?" She shook her head and looked away.

Drew wrestled his jeans on. "I'm different now, too, Laura. You just don't know it."

"Then that's one more thing that's my fault."

"I didn't say that."

"You didn't have to! It couldn't be more obvious. You were divorcing me. Leaving me. Scraping me off like gum from your shoe. Now that I'm different you want me back. It's like getting a brand-new woman for the price of the old one. And no one makes any moral judgments on you because, after all, I'm Mrs. Drew Bennett already."

"I never thought of you as gum," Drew said, almost laughing at the idiocy of the statement. "I mean, that analogy really misrepresents what happened between us. Ending our marriage was the most difficult decision I ever had to make."

"But you managed to do it." Her lips tightened into a line. "And you never answered my question. Nice evasion."

He knew exactly what she was referring to. "This is the last time I'm going to say this. There wasn't another woman. Unless you count you."

"What about my mother?"

"*What?*"

"I'm just trying to understand this," she said, fighting the tremor in her voice. "I don't see how you can sincerely want to be with someone after you fell so far out of love that the only answer was to break up the family."

"Things are different now. Or they were different then. For a while. By the time of the—" he stumbled over the words "—the accident, we were like different people. I didn't know who you were anymore."

"But now you do? Now that I don't know myself?"

"Yeah, I do. You're the woman I fell in love with."

Her face paled a shade. "You've only known me—*this* me—for less than a week." Her voice quieted.

"I've known you all my life."

Her stance remained defensive but her eyes betrayed her silent hope.

"Since I found you again, you've been the Laura I've loved for more than ten years." He searched for the words. "You've been open-minded and interested in things around you. We've had conversations and *listened* to each other instead of just talking *at* each other. We've been *friends* again. I missed that." He'd never said that before. "I missed it before you ever left."

She looked bemused. "What were we doing all that time then?"

"We were arguing. When I wasn't working and you weren't taking care of Sam, that is. It seemed like all we ever did was argue."

"About what?" She really looked as though she wanted to know. The defenses were down and her eyes showed that she was at least open to listening.

"You had grown so mistrustful that not a day passed without us fighting. I swear that there was no one else, but you were certain there was. There was nothing I could do to change your mind." His chest ached with remembered frustration. "It was a complete impasse."

The tension left her face. She looked defeated. "So

you started divorce proceedings.'' She sank to the bed.

He sat down and turned her by the shoulders to look her directly in the eye. "I couldn't take it anymore. It wasn't good for you or Samantha, either. I loved you, Laura, always. But our marriage reached a point where it was damaging us and, worse, Samantha.''

She looked down. "But you said we still loved each other and I believe that. Why couldn't we talk things over?''

He knew she wasn't going to like his answer. He didn't blame her. "I tried—or at least I thought I tried—but I didn't grow up putting much stock in talk.'' It was a lame excuse but it was the truth.

"But wasn't your father…''

He raised an eyebrow. "A psychiatrist. Yes. But talking to him meant having an expert manipulate the truth so you couldn't even give an answer to it.'' He laughed without humor and shook his head. "He was masterful.'' He leveled his gaze at Laura.

Her gaze hardened. "That doesn't justify lying.''

It felt like a slap in the face, just when he'd thought they were making progress. "I never lied to you.''

"You brought me home without telling me we were getting divorced.'' She braced her hands against the windowsill behind her.

"That wasn't a lie, it was an omission. Anyway, by the time I found you again, it wasn't even true.''

"You should have let me sort the facts and decide what was true and what wasn't for myself.''

He scoffed and leaned against the dresser. "Would it have made things easier for you if I'd said we were happy for years but things soured and we were going to get a divorce and then you died and I realized how wrong I'd been and that I should have tried harder to work things out with you, and if I'd only gotten one more chance I wouldn't have filed for divorce because I learned the hard way I couldn't live without you?" He paused for breath. "Would that have made things clearer for you?"

"At least it would have been the truth."

"The truth," he repeated. "I told you the truth. It was just an abbreviated version."

She gave a wry laugh. "And you criticize your father for manipulating the truth."

"Listen, sweetheart, you haven't been hugely forthcoming yourself. You barely spoke to me for *months* before you left."

"I must have had a good reason."

"What could possibly be a *good* reason for that?" Before she could interject he added, "You made negative assumptions about me instead of asking. Your whole damn family is like that. Newport blue bloods, too paranoid to ever give anyone the benefit of the doubt. You used to hate that."

"I hate it now," she countered. "Like your assumptions about what I can and cannot handle."

"Damn it!" He slammed his fist down on the dresser top. "Have you heard *anything* I've said to you?"

"Have *you* heard—"

"Daddy?" Samantha's voice at the door stopped them both cold. Drew felt all the blood drain from his face. He wouldn't have thought things could get worse, but this did it. Laura wasn't even home a week yet and poor Sam had to hear them fighting again.

He tried to brighten his expression. "Yes, Sam?" he asked, walking over to her.

She looked at Laura, then back at him. "Somebody's on the telephone for you." Her gaze flitted to the hallway phone, where Drew immediately realized the caller had probably heard every word he and Laura had said to each other since God knew when. He hadn't even heard the phone ring.

He heaved a sigh. "Thanks, honey." Without looking back at Laura he started for the door.

"Why are you and Mommy fighting?" Sam's small voice asked behind him.

He stopped short. "We're not—"

"I'll talk to her," Laura said in a strangely quiet voice. He met her eyes and she gave a nod toward the door. "You get the phone."

It was just as well, he decided, trying to keep from slamming the door shut. He knew from long experience that was an argument he couldn't win.

All he could do now was hope *she* had heard *him* this time.

When he had gone, Sam held out a book to Laura. "Will you read this to me?"

Laura took the book. *"Green Eggs and Ham,"* she read. "Is this one of your favorites?"

Sam nodded. "Yes."

"Well, let's take a look here." She led Sam to the bed and they sat down together, Sam nestled snugly in the crook of Laura's arm. Laura's heart pounded—this was familiar. This was a ritual she had loved.

"Are you going to read?" Sam asked, reaching across and flipping the pages with her chubby fingers. She stopped about halfway through the book, where there was a funny picture of green eggs and ham on a plate. "Read this page."

With a trepidation Laura couldn't understand, she swallowed and looked down at the page. "'I do not like green eggs and ham.'" Her breath left in a hard rush. The words on the page swam before her eyes.

"Keep reading!"

She moistened her parched lips and tried again. "'I do not like them, Sam I am.'"

Sam I am.

Sam I am.

The words echoed in her mind like pealing church bells. She tried to breathe but she couldn't. A dark cloud came over her mind, suffocating her, then, slowly, it started to lift.

Sam I am.

She smelled gasoline, and the stale smoky smell of a car, and the strong scent of cheap perfume, but it was memory, not real. It was a horrible memory—it made the back of her throat squeeze shut and her hands tremble—but unclear.

"Mommy, you stopped reading again." Sam's plaintive voice broke through the fog of Laura's consciousness.

She shut the book carefully, hoping Sam wouldn't notice her shaking hands. "I've just remembered something I have to do," she fudged. "Run to your room and play for a bit, okay?"

"You were going to read to me. You promised!"

"I know, but I'm tired." *Sam I am.* The words hummed in her head like a childish taunt. What did it mean?

"It's not late." Sam giggled. "Maybe you need a nap."

"Maybe I do." She leaned back and pressed the back of her hand to her forehead. It felt cool against her skin. She closed her eyes and tried to remember... Breakfast. She was in the kitchen running around to get Sam's breakfast to her, reciting the words to the book that lay open on the table...

I do not like them, Sam I am.

"Mommy has to go, Sammy. She has an appointment. Come on now, finish your applesauce."

"Are you going to finish the book first?" Sam asked.

"I'll read to you tonight." Sam needed to be occupied for a while, so Laura could gather herself. "Why don't you go take out every book you have that has a brown horse on the cover." She knew she'd seen at least two books with horses on them. "Can you do that?"

This task apparently satisfied Sam's urge for games. "Just brown horses?"

"Just brown."

"Okay." She smiled and gave Laura a hard hug before skipping toward the door, and nearly running headlong into Drew.

He barely seemed to notice—he just patted her shoulder and murmured something unintelligible to her. He was more pale than Laura had ever seen him. The news over the phone must have been horrible. His movements were mechanical, the look in his eyes was blank.

"What's happened?" Laura asked him.

He stood motionless. "That was the police chief. They exhumed the body in your grave." He glanced at Laura and quickly added, "I'm sorry, I shouldn't have said it that way. Those are words no one should ever hear.''

Laura trembled violently. She hadn't thought about the woman in the grave in a long time. ''They exhumed it today?''

''No. They've been doing tests, trying to confirm the identity.''

Laura's stomach twisted. She tried to speak but couldn't. An ocean of silence filled the space between them as they looked at each other. She swallowed, then swallowed again, twining and untwining her fingers before her. ''I'm afraid to ask.''

''Gena Finley.'' He looked away, then shook his head. Finally he looked back at her. ''She was the woman you asked me about when you were looking through the business cards on my desk.''

She recalled that incident but—this? She didn't understand it. She felt like she was on the verge of something but she couldn't tell whether it was remembering her past or getting sick. Gena Finley was in a grave marked Laura Bennett. It didn't make sense but, to her horror, it didn't surprise her, either. Why? ''What...'' She searched for the words since the memory wasn't there. ''How...could they tell?''

''When I told the police you were alive, they went back and did a more thorough investigation. The day of the accident Gena's car was found abandoned. A few days after that, she was reported missing but it never occurred to them it could have anything to do with a death in Connecticut.''

''So how did they?''

''They took a chance and got her dental records. It was the only viable means of identification. And it worked.''

Laura nodded slowly, swallowing hard at the lump in her throat. "But what does she have to do with us? Or you, or me. Was she a friend of mine?"

He let out a long breath. "No. I worked with her. She was a colleague, not a close friend."

Gena Finley. Who was that? What did that mean to her? *Gena. Gena Finley.* It sounded familiar now. Was that because of the business card? She took a couple of aimless steps away. "I don't understand this."

Drew walked numbly to the chair and sat down, slinging his arm across the copy of *The Ghost and Mrs. Muir* Laura had picked up her first day there. Ghosts—both living and dead—seemed to be the theme of their lives lately.

She went to him and he looked up at her with pain in his expression. "I'm sorry," he said.

"Why? Drew, what's the significance here?" Laura's heart rate escalated with every word. "You said you barely knew the woman."

He held her gaze. "That's true—she was only a co-worker, and in a different office at that. I might have seen her one or two times a week at the most."

"Okay." Laura cocked her head, waiting for a further explanation.

He hesitated. "There's just...one more thing."

Something inside Laura recoiled. This was important, she knew, but she didn't want any more revelations. Part of her just wanted to run away, run back to Connecticut and resume her life as Mary Shepherd. But she couldn't do that now. She had to face it all. "What is it?"

"First you have to understand one thing. I didn't tell you because there was no point in making things any more convoluted by adding names.'' He took a long breath and tightened his lips. ''I didn't think it was significant. Now, of course, I see that it was.''

Laura shifted her weight and shrugged impatiently. ''What? What is it?''

He looked at her directly. ''You weren't just convinced I was having an affair,'' he said, his voice ringing with an unspoken fear. ''You were convinced I was having an affair with Gena Finley.''

Chapter Ten

"Oh, dear Lord," Laura gasped, clapping a trembling hand to her mouth.

"I should have been more patient with your fears, no matter how unfounded they were," Drew said, coming to her.

The trembling spread across her entire body and hummed in her ears like a helicopter landing. "Drew." She leaned into his outstretched arms, and turned her eyes to him. She had to force herself not to look away when she asked, "Do you think I killed her?"

There was no way he could have faked the shock in his eyes. "Do I think *you* killed her?" He laughed a hearty laugh that contrasted so sharply with the mood that it reassured Laura more than words could possibly have. "Of course not. You would never even think of doing something like that."

She searched his eyes, frantically trying to recall the face of the woman on the business card, and the images that had nudged at her consciousness when she saw it. Blond hair. Pale eyes. *Gena.*

"This is Gena Finley. We need to talk."

"Surely you know yourself better than to think you're capable of that," Drew was saying.

What were all these words suddenly echoing in her head? "I...I think so," she managed.

"Look." He took her firmly by the shoulders and looked into her eyes. "There's obviously a connection of some sort since Gena was in your car, apparently wearing your wedding band and watch, and whatever else you had. But I know one thing, *you* were not at fault for whatever happened."

She wished she could believe that as fully as he did. "But what—" *Sam I am.* Suddenly she felt dizzy. When she put her hand to her forehead, she found she had broken out in a sweat. "What was she doing..."

"It's okay," Drew said, gently easing her over to the chair. "Here you go." He lowered her into it, and sat on the floor in front of her, holding both her hands in his. His watch was hard against her thigh but somehow that one physical sensation kept her feeling sane.

"Take the worst-case scenario," Drew said, rubbing his thumbs across the tops of her hands. "You hate her, you want her dead. Why would you dress her up in your clothes, put your wedding ring and watch on her, leave your purse and other incidentals with her and send her off to her doom? For that matter, how could you even have known she *was* driving off to her doom? You weren't even in the car."

He had a point but it didn't explain the unavoidable facts. "But it *was* my car and my clothes, and everything else. I obviously had *something* to do with it."

Heat melted over her, leaving icy cold in its wake. "But what?" *Gena Finley. Gena.*

"Drew's mine now. You don't belong in his life anymore. Why couldn't you just leave him alone and let us be happy? If you had left us alone none of this would be necessary."

"Oh, no." Laura's grip on Drew's hands tightened. She tried to stop the cacophony of voices that had long ago buried themselves in her subconscious, only to be resurrected in this mad rush.

"What is it?" Drew asked.

Laura took deep steady breaths, remembering the technique of floating with stress instead of fighting against it. "I think...I can hear it."

"Hear what?"

She closed her eyes tightly and spoke the images that came to her. "Gena Finley. She called. On the phone, that phone in the library. I was in the library...." She could see the black phone and the scuff marks she'd been intending to polish off. When it rang that day and she reached for it, and chastised herself for the hundredth time about the scuff marks.

"It's all right, take your time," Drew reassured her.

"Meet me at the Port Authority. I'm leaving town and I want to tell you the truth before I go."

"She wanted me to meet her. Talk to her. She said she wanted to tell me about the two of you." Her heart banged against her rib cage. "I went to meet her, and..."

"How could we possibly have a chance with you there all the time? Laura this, Laura that, Drew's beautiful wife, Laura. It was sickening."

"She said you were angry because I wouldn't let you go."

"He'll probably have to act the part of the grieving widower for a little while, but I'll be there to help him through. Don't you worry about that. And I'll take care of our little girl, too, our little Samantha. People say she looks like me, but I think she's much more like her father...."

"I never spoke to her about anything more personal than opening a new office in Seattle." His voice was hard.

Laura looked at him, only half seeing for the obstruction of the past. "She'd been calling for months." Laura leveled her gaze on Drew. "She knew *everything* about you. Knew every hotel you'd stayed in, every restaurant you'd eaten at in other towns. I checked the credit card receipts. She was right and she knew it all."

Drew remained in stunned silence for several seconds before saying, "All of that was on my expense report. It would have been easy for her to get the information. But why would she do that? Why would she care?"

Laura gave a dry laugh. "She was in love with you, Drew. Or obsessed with you anyway. She saw me as the one obstacle between the two of you, so she set out to get rid of me."

"By making it look like I was having an affair with her?" He didn't look convinced. "How could she make you believe that?"

Laura studied his eyes and saw guileless truth there. "I guess things aren't always what they seem, huh?"

"But common sense—"

"You believed I was dead without so much as a dental record."

He cocked his head slightly to the side. "All right. You may have a point there."

Laura let out a long breath, still reeling at the facts. "It seemed so real, so convincing until she started acting so irrationally. But now the truth is just as clear, I just wasn't seeing it then."

Drew pinched the bridge of his nose with his thumb and index finger. "And I wasn't helping any because I figured you should have known me better than that, and if you didn't believe in me on your own there was no way I could change your mind." He thumped his palm against his forehead. "I could have prevented all of this."

Laura shook her head slowly, still pulling the threads apart in her mind. "I don't think so. I drew my conclusions on my own, despite what my heart told me about you. After all those years of trying to be different from the rest of my family, trying to avoid making assumptions and taking drastic actions, I nearly got myself killed by being just like them."

Drew's features were drawn. "I should have tried harder to find out what was happening."

"Maybe." She shrugged. "But maybe it wouldn't have changed anything." She rubbed her eyes. "We weren't the only ones involved at this point. That woman..."

He raked his hand across his hair. "Do you know what else happened? How you ended up in Connecticut?"

"I know she drove," Laura remembered. "She had a gun. She forced me over and drove on to the ferry." She gave a wry laugh. "It was so easy for her. We crossed to Cape Cod in the car carrier. It was dark, smelled of burning oil. She told me all about the things she was going to do with my life when it was hers." She shuddered at the thought.

He pulled her closer. "Oh, Laura."

Laura looked toward the window. "I tried not to listen. I'd been reading to Sam over breakfast. *Green Eggs and Ham.* I kept thinking that phrase, *Sam I am,* over and over again." She gave a dry laugh. "A mad woman's got a gun pointed at my ribs and all I can think of is 'Sam I am' over and over like a mantra. It's been stuck in my head ever since. Just now, when I read it to Sam, it's as though it unlocked something."

He chuckled softly but she heard the concern behind it. "Maybe that was the one bridge across your amnesia." He paused. "Do you remember anything else?"

She returned her attention to that day, like turning her gaze to the passing clouds. "She took my clothes, switched with me. Then she tied my wrists and ankles so I wouldn't jump out of the car. She did that on the ferry, then covered me with a blanket so they wouldn't see the ropes when we drove off. The blanket smelled like gasoline." Laura shivered convulsively. "She took my wedding ring and she put it on her finger."

"This is mine. I'm Mrs. Drew Bennett, not you. I've waited a long time to wear Drew Bennett's wedding ring. Of course it's a perfect fit."

"She put all my things on, she took my purse, she was driving my car." Laura listed the inventory with perfect clarity. "She really thought she was me. She thought she could just erase me and insert herself into my place."

Drew pulled her hand to his lips, then pressed it against his cheek. "Take it easy, Laura. Don't push. I don't want you to make yourself ill."

She focused on him. He was beautiful. Thick dark hair, intense brown eyes, that sexy shadow of dark razor stubble. He had always been beautiful. "Ill?" she repeated with a laugh. "Satch, I haven't felt this good since... Jeez, since that night in Aruba with the piña coladas, and..."

He looked at her with the same expression he'd had the first day he'd seen her back in Nantucket and she realized, only then, that it had all come back to her. The details of Gena Finley's attack were foggy, but her life was back in place as if it had never gone amiss.

"You remember Aruba?" he asked incredulously.

"I do remember," she said, a little amazed herself. Her memory was like a boat maneuvering neatly back into a slip.

She stood up, opened a drawer in the night table and reached in. "Wow, it's still here." She pulled a string of colorful beads out of the drawer. "Remember?"

"Yes," he said slowly, looking at the dangling beads. He met her eyes. "I told you someday I'd get you real diamonds."

She smiled, tears burning in her eyes. "I'm still waiting." She gave a laugh and a sniff. Truth was, she wouldn't have traded the beads for anything. Drew had given them to her on a secluded beach at sunset. He'd been tanned as brown as a walnut. He looked like a pirate, with an almost-sinister sketch of beard and brown skin creased with wicked laugh lines.

"Do you remember everything?" Drew asked.

"I don't know but...I remember enough." She smiled at him and touched her fingers to a tear on his cheek. "I remember you. And I know that I made horrible, unforgivable mistakes with our marriage."

"*You?* I was the one—"

"Shh." She put a finger on his lips. "I wanted to tell you before—I knew it as soon as I saw her that day—but I didn't get the chance. The real reason I believed you were having an affair was because I knew—I *knew* this, Drew—that I had stopped being the woman you married. I felt boring, out of shape, ugly...."

He looked shocked. "You weren't. None of that is true."

"It was true enough to start me hating myself and blaming you." She shook her head, holding his gaze steady with her eyes. "It was pretty hard to believe you'd want to be with me when I couldn't stand being with myself." She swallowed. "I thought I'd lost myself and I didn't know how to get it back." She gave a wry chuckle. "Little did I know..."

"I should have known," Drew said. "I should have seen, but I didn't. I should have helped."

"You couldn't," she said emphatically. "My mental state was mine alone. No one could have changed my mind except me and, unfortunately, it took me just a little too long to do it." She pressed her lips together and touched his cheek. "But I know now, I understand now, what I put you through by indulging my petty insecurities. I was so selfish, Drew. How on earth could you want to take me back?"

"Funny, I spent all that time wondering how on earth I could let you go." He smiled. "I couldn't."

"Maybe you should have."

"What, and missed this reunion? You've got to be kidding."

She smiled, but sobered quickly and said, "Please believe me, I'll never make that mistake again." Her eyes filled with tears. "We must never take each other for granted again."

He was upon her in an instant, practically devouring her with hungry kisses, which she returned in equal measure.

She ran her fingers through his hair, across his shoulders, his back, his ribs—everywhere. In a way it felt like moments since she'd last touched him, but in another way it felt like years.

Long minutes passed as they clutched at each other like two teenagers in the back of a car, unable to get enough of each other.

"Wait," Laura said, pulling back slightly.

"I *have* been," he answered, kissing her again. His tongue touched the tip of hers and she went weak, breathing into him, sinking into him, moving as close as humanly possible.

She lingered within the sensation for only a few seconds before drawing back again. "Seriously, Drew."

"I'm *really serious,* Laura." He pressed his proof against her leg and she felt her knees start to buckle.

"There are more important things to think about right now," she told him, trying to hold back a smile.

His expression clouded for a moment, then cleared. "Sam."

She nodded, unable to keep her laughter in check.

"I can't wait to tell her I'm really and truly back for her." She traced her finger down his chest. "We can finish this later...?"

"Bet on it," he said.

They started out of the room then Drew stopped. "Now that you're really back, I've got to ask you something."

"What?"

He grinned devilishly. "What's for dinner?"

She eyed him for a moment then started walking. "I don't cook."

"Yes, you do."

"Really? I don't remember."

"Laura, come on. We are *really* sick of hot dogs and beans."

She stopped and turned to face him. "Is that what you've been feeding my daughter? Hot dogs and beans?"

He paused. "Not always."

"Good."

"Friday is pizza night."

She gasped. "Drew Bennett, you are pitiful. Remind me never to leave you alone with that child for any length of time again."

He captured her in an embrace and planted a long, slow kiss on her lips. "I promise. From now on you're not going away without us."

"And you?" she asked, suddenly serious. "Can you promise that you'll be home more now?"

He held her gaze for a long moment, then said, "I'm standing right by your side, loving you for the rest of your life."

"We have a deal." She smiled. "I'll hold you to it. And this time I'm not going to forget. Ever."

Epilogue

Epilogue

The small tap at the door echoed through the bathroom.

"Mommy?" The door creaked open and Sam poked her head around the corner. "We brought you a Mother's Day breakfast in bed."

Even though she'd been back with her family for more than a year now, every time Laura saw her daughter she was grateful for the coincidences that brought her back to Nantucket after her long, dark period of amnesia.

"That's sweet, honey." She pushed herself up off the cold tile floor. "I'm coming."

"Sam?" The door swung open a little wider and Laura saw her husband, handsome as sin, even in his Saturday T-shirt and sweatpants. As soon as he saw Laura, a sympathetic light came into his eyes. "Sam, why don't you run downstairs and pour Mommy a ginger ale?"

"For *breakfast?*" Sam giggled. "Okay. Mother's

Day sure is a crazy day.'' She skipped out of the room.

As soon as she was gone, Drew put a hand out to Laura. ''Morning sickness no better?''

She smiled weakly. ''It's just the first three months. I was like this with Sam, too. The doctor swore it meant the baby is healthy.''

He put his arm around Laura's shoulder to steady her and led her back to the bed. ''I wish I could do something to help.''

''You've done quite enough, thank you.'' Laura laughed. ''But I wouldn't mind seven more months of major pampering.'' She sat down on the edge of the bed and leaned back into the pillows. He sat down on the edge of the bed by her. ''If it wouldn't be too much trouble.''

''Trouble? Nah.'' Drew smiled and it made her heart flip. Just as it had done the first time she'd ever seen him. He rested his head gently on her belly and looked into her eyes. ''It's a small price to pay for the gift you're giving me.''

''What's Mommy giving you?'' Sam said from the doorway. ''Do I get something, too?''

''As a matter of fact, you do,'' Laura said. ''This gift is for all of us and we're going to get it right around Christmastime.''

''What is it?'' Sam asked excitedly, setting the plastic cartoon cup of ginger ale on the table next to Laura.

Drew pulled his daughter into his arms and said, ''How would you like a baby brother or sister?''

Sam's eyes lit up. ''*Really?* Is that the gift?''

''That's the gift.''

"Oh, boy!" Sam wriggled out of Drew's arms and danced around the room. "Can I name him?"

"What makes you so sure it's going to be a boy?" Laura asked.

"Because that's what I asked Santa Claus for last Christmas. He said he couldn't bring a baby on his sleigh because it was too cold outside, but I knew he would do it, I just knew."

Drew smiled at Laura and hummed a few bars of "I saw Mommy Kissing Santa Claus" and they both laughed.

"I'm going to have a brother or a sister," Sam sang happily.

"And what did you ask Santa for last year?" Laura asked Drew over the noise of Sam's exuberance.

"I don't ask for anything anymore." He leaned over and kissed her lips, then ran his thumb along the line of her jaw, a gesture so familiar to her that it made her sigh. "I don't need to."

She swallowed and looked into his eyes. "Why not? Don't you want anything?"

He shook his head and glanced at Sam, who was still dancing wildly about the room. "Ever since you came back I've got it all."

* * * * *

Look for Elizabeth Harbison's next delightful Silhouette Romance title, TWO BROTHERS AND A BRIDE, coming in March 1998.

ELIZABETH AUGUST

Continues the twelve-book series—36 HOURS—in November 1997 with Book Five

CINDERELLA STORY

Life was hardly a fairy tale for Nina Lindstrom. Out of work and with an ailing child, the struggling single mom was running low on hope. Then Alex Bennett solved her problems with one convenient proposal: marriage. And though he had made no promises beyond financial security, Nina couldn't help but feel that with a little love, happily-ever-afters really could come true!

For Alex and Nina and *all* the residents of Grand Springs, Colorado, the storm-induced blackout was just the beginning of 36 Hours that changed *everything!* You won't want to miss a single book.

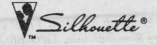

Take 4 bestselling love stories FREE

Plus get a FREE surprise gift!

Special Limited-time Offer

Mail to Silhouette Reader Service™

3010 Walden Avenue
P.O. Box 1867
Buffalo, N.Y. 14240-1867

YES! Please send me 4 free Silhouette Romance™ novels and my free surprise gift. Then send me 6 brand-new novels every month, which I will receive months before they appear in bookstores. Bill me at the low price of $2.67 each plus 25¢ delivery and applicable sales tax, if any.* That's the complete price and a savings of over 10% off the cover prices—quite a bargain! I understand that accepting the books and gift places me under no obligation ever to buy any books. I can always return a shipment and cancel at any time. Even if I never buy another book from Silhouette, the 4 free books and the surprise gift are mine to keep forever.

215 BPA A3UT

Name	(PLEASE PRINT)	
Address	Apt. No.	
City	State	Zip

This offer is limited to one order per household and not valid to present Silhouette Romance™ subscribers. *Terms and prices are subject to change without notice. Sales tax applicable in N.Y.

USROM-696   ©1990 Harlequin Enterprises Limited

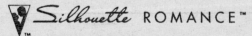

Bundles of Joy

Babies have a way of bringing out the love in
everyone's hearts! And Silhouette Romance
is delighted to present you with three
wonderful new love stories.

October:

DADDY WOKE UP MARRIED by Julianna Morris (SR#1252)

Emily married handsome Nick Carleton temporarily to give her unborn child
a name. Then a tumble off the roof left this amnesiac daddy-to-be thinking
lovely Emily was his *real* wife, and was she enjoying it! But what would
happen when Nick regained his memory?

December:

THE BABY CAME C.O.D. by Marie Ferrarella (SR#1264)

(Two Halves of a Whole)

Tycoon Evan Quartermain found a *baby* in his office—with a note saying the
adorable little girl was his! Luckily next-door neighbor and pretty single mom
Claire was glad to help out, and soon Evan was forgoing corporate takeovers
in favor of baby rattles and long, sultry nights with the beautiful Claire!

February:

Silhouette Romance is pleased to present ON BABY PATROL by
Sharon DeVita, (SR#1276), which is also the first of her new
Lullabies and Love series. A legendary cradle brings the three rugged
Sullivan brothers unexpected love, fatherhood and family.

Don't miss these adorable Bundles of Joy, only from

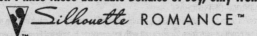

As seen on TV!
Free Gift Offer

With a Free Gift proof-of-purchase from any Silhouette® book,
you can receive a beautiful cubic zirconia pendant.

This gorgeous marquise-shaped stone is a genuine cubic
zirconia—accented by an 18" gold tone necklace.

(Approximate retail value $19.95)

Send for yours today...
compliments of 🌹 *Silhouette*®
TM

To receive your free gift, a cubic zirconia pendant, send us one original proof-of-purchase, photocopies not accepted, from the back of any Silhouette Romance™, Silhouette Desire®, Silhouette Special Edition®, Silhouette Intimate Moments® or Silhouette Yours Truly™ title available at your favorite retail outlet, together with the Free Gift Certificate, plus a check or money order for $1.65 U.S./$2.15 CAN. (do not send cash) to cover postage and handling, payable to Silhouette Free Gift Offer. We will send you the specified gift. Allow 6 to 8 weeks for delivery. Offer good until December 31, 1997, or while quantities last. Offer valid in the U.S. and Canada only.

Free Gift Certificate

Name: _____

Address: _____

City: _____ State/Province: _____ Zip/Postal Code: _____

Mail this certificate, one proof-of-purchase and a check or money order for postage and handling to: SILHOUETTE FREE GIFT OFFER 1997. In the U.S.: 3010 Walden Avenue, P.O. Box 9077, Buffalo NY 14269-9077. In Canada: P.O. Box 613, Fort Erie, Ontario L2Z 5X3.

FREE GIFT OFFER   084-KFD

ONE PROOF-OF-PURCHASE

To collect your fabulous FREE GIFT, a cubic zirconia pendant, you must include this
original proof-of-purchase for each gift with the properly completed Free Gift Certificate.

084-KFDR

SILHOUETTE WOMEN KNOW ROMANCE WHEN THEY SEE IT.

And they'll see it on **ROMANCE CLASSICS**, the new 24-hour TV channel devoted to romantic movies and original programs like the special **Romantically Speaking—Harlequin™ Goes Prime Time.**

Romantically Speaking—Harlequin™ Goes Prime Time introduces you to many of your favorite romance authors in a program developed exclusively for Harlequin® and Silhouette® readers.

Watch for **Romantically Speaking—Harlequin™ Goes Prime Time** beginning in the summer of 1997.

If you're not receiving ROMANCE CLASSICS, call your local cable operator or satellite provider and ask for it today!

ROMANCE CLASSICS

Escape to the network of your dreams.

See Ingrid Bergman and Gregory Peck in *Spellbound* on Romance Classics.

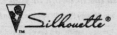